The ice prin

For *him.*

Maddy kissed him frantically, tangling her fingers in the hair at the nape of his neck. Jake instinctively dropped his hands, reaching for the round curves of her backside that he'd been admiring since they met. Cupping those curves, he savored their softness, squeezing her lightly. He was going to love holding her cheeks tightly when she was naked and on top of him. Plunging down onto him, over and over, until he lost his mind and exploded inside her.

Tugging her up for a nicer fit, he rocked into her, letting her feel his throbbing erection, getting off at the pleasure of·sex against sex, despite their clothes.

She whimpered, tilting her hips against him to bring her heat directly against the seam straining to hold back his arousal. "I want you so much," she rasped.

"I noticed." He spun her around, backing her against the building. It was crazy—they were outside, in a public place. It wasn't even ten o'clock and anyone could walk out of the bar any minute. But he didn't care. If he didn't get more of her, he'd die. "Please don't stop me..." he whispered hoarsely as his lips nudged her blouse aside to reveal a hint of her breast rising above the edge of a hot-pink bra.

"Stopping you isn't even a consideration."

Blaze™

Dear Reader,

I loved writing books for the Harlequin Temptation line as much as I love writing books for Harlequin Blaze now. And when I found out my very favorite Temptation miniseries—THE WRONG BED—was being brought over to Blaze, I *knew* I would have to write one.

Or two!

Having had my Harlequin Temptation couples end up in the wrong beds because of mixed-up room keys, confusing twins and mischievous ghosts, I wanted to find a unique way to bring them together in Harlequin Blaze. And a foul-up at a bachelor auction—where an all-American rescue worker is mistaken for an international gigolo...and vice versa—seemed like a fun way to do it.

So here you'll meet Jake. Supersexy, supernice, superheroic boy next door, who simply cannot believe it when über-rich Madeleine Turner offers him a small fortune to be "hers" for one month. And next month you must come back to read Sean Donovan's story...international playboy meets down-home family out on the farm. You won't want to miss it!

Hope you enjoy these Wrong Beds...Again and Again!

Best wishes,

Leslie Kelly

LESLIE KELLY
Slow Hands

HARLEQUIN®

TORONTO • NEW YORK • LONDON
AMSTERDAM • PARIS • SYDNEY • HAMBURG
STOCKHOLM • ATHENS • TOKYO • MILAN • MADRID
PRAGUE • WARSAW • BUDAPEST • AUCKLAND

ISBN-13: 978-0-373-79406-5
ISBN-10:   0-373-79406-1

SLOW HANDS

Copyright © 2008 by Leslie Kelly.

This edition published by arrangement with Harlequin Books S.A.

® and TM are trademarks of the publisher. Trademarks indicated with ® are registered in the United States Patent and Trademark Office, the Canadian Trade Marks Office and in other countries.

www.eHarlequin.com

Printed in U.S.A.

ABOUT THE AUTHOR

A two-time RWA RITA® Award nominee, eight-time *Romantic Times BOOKreviews* Award nominee and 2006 *Romantic Times BOOKreviews* Award winner, Leslie Kelly has become known for her delightful characters, sparkling dialogue and outrageous humor. Since the publication of her first book in 1999, Leslie has gone on to pen more than two dozen sassy, sexy romances. Honored with numerous other awards, including the National Readers' Choice Award, Leslie writes sexy novels for Harlequin Blaze, and single-title contemporaries for HQN Books. Keep up with her latest releases by visiting her Web site, www.lesliekelly.com, or her blog, www.plotmonkeys.com.

To the fabulous Plotmonkeys gang, including
Katie, Jodie, Paula, Donna, Pat, Jeannie
(and Zoey!), Tina, Kelly, Cher, Ev, Vero, Ardie,
Jane, Estella, Elisa, Fedora, Kim, Stacy, Kathy,
Bailey, Jaci, Patty, Michelle, Liza, Shari, Cherylann
and so many more. Hanging out with all of you in
The Jungle makes me smile every single day. Thank
you so much for your friendship and support!

Prologue

"OH, MY GOD, I CAN'T DO THIS, it's hopeless! We're not going to be able to pull it off."

Penny Rausch heard the panic in her partner's voice and struggled to keep her own alarm under control. One of them had to stay calm. Otherwise they were both going to lose their minds…not to mention their fledgling graphic design business.

"Calm down. We're almost there."

Janice, her partner and more-than-slightly ditzy younger sister, thrust her hand into her spiked blond hair, sending it into even more crazy directions than it had been before. A highly sought-after graphic designer, Janice had no head for business, but wow, was the girl creative…and not just with her hair. Her graphics were incredible. Her drawings collectible. Her fashion sense wildly imaginative.

Too bad she was pretty helpless in nearly every other aspect of her life.

"I dropped the file. The last six photos went everywhere. Just shoot me now."

She looked utterly exhausted, with dark circles under her eyes and a haggard hollowness in her cheeks. Janice was usually very precise about her appearance, but right now her yellow T-shirt was stained with something that was either ketchup from today's fries or tomato sauce from last night's pizza.

They hadn't left their office in thirty-six hours. Not since

Janice's expensive, nearly brand-new computer had crashed, taking most of the files for the high-end, glossy brochure they were producing down with it. And almost taking down their company, too.

Because if they lost this job—creating the programs for a ritzy charity bachelor auction scheduled for next week—they were finished. They wouldn't make the already-late rent, or keep the power on, or cover the printing bill. They'd be out of business overnight, after only being *in* it for eight months.

"We can handle this," Penny insisted. "We've come this far, we're almost there."

"Maybe we could contact Mrs. Baxter…"

"No. Absolutely impossible." They could not let the snooty Junior League socialite know they'd had yet *another* mishap in the design job. No way. They were already on probation, thanks to a few hiccups—like Janice's case of the flu and a flood in the office. If they admitted to the computer crash, the woman would kick them to the curb for good.

"I can't even tell them apart anymore," Janice wailed, waving toward the table laden with photographs and copy. "Looking at one gorgeous man after another, hour after hour…"

"Tough job."

"It's not funny. I thought we were in the clear when we found the backup set of hard copies. *Why* didn't we put the bachelors' info on the back when we made them?"

The biographies of the bachelors being auctioned off to support Chicago's needy children had been on the backs of the originals. But the originals had gone back to the penny-pinching auction organizer, Mrs. Baxter, once they'd been copied and scanned. Now they had the scans on disc, and they had the hard duplicates. They even had the printed biographies.

They just didn't have any of those things *together.* And they had no way of knowing who was who.

If not for some easily identifiable, well-known bachelors, some handwritten notes, as well as Google, which they'd accessed on Penny's still-working laptop, they would have had to give up. But not now. *We're not giving up now.*

"We're down to those last six men, Janice," Penny insisted, bending to pick over the spilled photos. She laid them out on the worktable, grabbing the small index cards with the bios. "And I just identified four of them."

Janice's eyes widened in delight. "Really?"

Penny nodded, putting the correct bio cards with the correct faces, clipping them together in case there were any more spills. "I have spent the past five hours looking at archives in the *Trib* and I've found more of our boys. Eligible bachelors apparently get a lot of press coverage."

Janice threw her arms around Penny and squeezed her. "So we're down to these last two."

Yes. Just two. "But we're out of time. We have less than an hour to get the whole package to the printer's if we're going to make the deadline." *No more time to research…no more hesitation.*

Penny lifted the two photographs, studying the handsome faces carefully. Both were dark-haired, but that was where the resemblance ended. One had warm brown eyes, the other vivid blue. One's hair was short and conservative, the other's a little longer, almost brushing his collar. One had a dangerous glint in his eye, the other a sexy smile on his curved lips.

"One is a paramedic, the other an international businessman," Penny whispered, knowing their bios by heart. "One of you is Jake and one of you is Sean."

Janice came closer, looking over Penny's shoulder. Penny could almost feel her sister's heartbeat just inches from her arm. She could *definitely* hear her deep, quick inhalations.

This was the moment—she had to choose. Suddenly remembering that old Lady or the Tiger story from her school days, she drew in a deep breath and pointed to the unsmiling one with the short hair and brown eyes. "He's got to be the businessman."

Beside her, Janice immediately nodded, pointing toward the other picture with the smiling, longer-haired guy. "And that's a strong rescue worker if I ever saw one."

"So we're agreed?"

"Agreed. Absolutely. No doubt about it."

Then it was done. Penny clipped the bios to the back of each picture, glad her sister was just as confident as she was that they'd made the right choice. Then she sat down to finish up the program on her own, older computer. And as she typed away as fast as she could, incorporating the newly recreated graphics, she tried hard to pretend she didn't hear her younger sister's whisper.

"I hope."

1

"OUR STEPMOMMY DEAREST is about to buy herself a gigolo."

Madeline Turner, who'd been signing a foot-tall stack of documents at her desk, dropped her pen, leaving a blot of black ink on the second quarter Profit and Loss Statement from a major local firm. Looking up, she could muster no surprise when she realized her sharp-toned visitor was her older half sister, Tabitha, looking as enraged as she sounded.

Enraged...but beautiful, as always. The stunning fashion plate had inherited all her mother's tall and slender genes, blond hair and elegance, which suited her lifestyle to a T. Madeline, meanwhile, had been gifted with their father's more short and round frame, plus her late mother's nearly black hair; dark, laughing eyes and dimples. Which did *not* suit her lifestyle as a nose-to-the-grindstone bank manager to an R or a squiggly S, much less to a T.

Tabitha tossed her designer handbag onto an empty chair and kicked the door shut with the heel of one pointy-toed, five-hundred-dollar shoe. "Maddy, did you hear me?"

"I think the construction workers twenty floors down heard you," Madeline mumbled, wondering why Tabitha always had to be so damned melodramatic. Something else she'd inherited from her jet-setting mother.

"The money-grubbing witch is going to cheat on our father."

Considering Tabitha had cheated on one of her husbands *and* one of her fiancés, Maddy figured her sister had better jump off that moral high ground upon which she was perched before it crumbled out from underneath her. Still she frowned, not happy with the news that their father's newest wife—his fourth—was already looking around for more adventure than her older husband could provide.

Tabby might loathe Deborah, but Maddy had never had anything against her. The woman wasn't exactly warmth personified, especially not to her adult stepdaughters, but she was a lot better than some of the alternatives. Their father could have married a twenty-five-year old…someone younger than Maddy or her sister. At least Deborah, aside from being in her forties, was well-spoken, graceful and successful. She had once run her own successful ballroom dancing studio—that's where she'd met Maddy's father—and seemed to make him happy, first as a dance partner, now as a wife.

So she really hoped Tabby was wrong. "How do you know this?"

"I got it straight from Bitsy Wellington."

Their stepmother's best gal pal. "Why would she tell *you*?"

"Well, you know Bitsy. She can never resist causing trouble."

True. The woman was completely toxic.

"Besides, she wants the man for herself. He's some European gigolo being auctioned off at that Give A Kid A Christmas charity gig at the InterContinental tomorrow night."

A gigolo being sold to benefit a children's charity. There was some serious irony in that. Leave it to the Ladies Who Lunch of Chicago to come up with the idea of buying a stud to raise money for a worthy cause. And then, to compete over him.

Tabitha lowered herself to one of the chairs across from Maddy's broad desk, sniffing slightly at the messy files strewn across it. Her big sister liked the money that came from the bank their great-grandfather had founded several decades ago. She just didn't particularly like the stench of work that came along with it.

Sometimes Maddy wondered if one of them had been adopted. Or found on a doorstep. They had *so* little in common with each other, physically as well as everything else.

In personality, she was told she was a lot like her mother, Jason Turner's second wife, who'd died when Maddy was four. Supposedly, though he never spoke of her, Jason had mourned her greatly. Which could explain why her sister always harassed Maddy about being their father's favorite.

Maybe it was just that they had more in common. Aside from looking more like Jason than Tabby did, Maddy was also blessed with his quick mind, one fascinated by banking and finance. She also had the work ethic to run the business that had been in the family for generations.

That didn't mean Tabitha hadn't gotten something from their father, too—his fickleness. Maddy seemed to be the only Turner who didn't fall in and out of love as frequently as the networks changed their Friday night lineup.

"We have to *do* something."

"About what?"

"About the little cheater, that's what!"

Maddy sighed, lowered her pen, and leaned back in her chair. "But she hasn't cheated yet, has she?"

"No…and we're going to make damn sure she doesn't."

Frankly, her sister's attitude came as a surprise. Considering how strongly Tabitha disliked their father's new wife, Maddy would have figured Tabitha would want Deborah to cheat, and get *caught*. Her father would tolerate a lot when it came to his wives—spending money, demanding attention and throwing tantrums. But he would never tolerate being cheated on. As a few of his former loves could certainly attest. Tabitha's mother included.

"I'm surprised you haven't hired a detective to follow her and get the goods yourself."

Tabitha frowned, shifting her pretty blue eyes away to study her perfectly manicured nails.

"You have? Jesus, Tabby…"

"Look, it was stupid, and I changed my mind almost right away. I don't want to catch the bitch cheating."

"You don't?"

Her sister finally lifted her eyes, and in them was a hint of genuineness, an emotion Tabitha didn't often let the world see, but which Maddy knew lurked beneath her sister's polished, shiny, brittle surface. "He loves her, Mad. Really loves her and she makes him so happy. It's like he's twenty years younger." She swallowed, murmuring, "I don't want him hurt. *Again.*"

Wow. That stunned her. So much that she couldn't reply for a minute. Because while she completely understood the sentiment—and felt the same way—she wouldn't have expected it of Tabitha.

Then she remembered the one area where she and her sister were absolutely, one hundred percent alike: in their love for their father.

She lowered her pen to her desk, finally giving her sister her undivided attention. "Okay. What do you propose we do?"

Tabitha dissembled for a moment, glancing around the room, at the few framed photos on Maddy's bookshelf—all family— at the plants in the corner and the view of the Chicago skyline out the window.

She wasn't going to like this, Maddy knew. Tabitha had the same look she'd had when they were nine and twelve and her big sister had suggested they "borrow" their new stepmother's— wife three's—Dior gowns to play house. And Maddy had the same reaction—the similar twitch in her temple and the sweatiness in her palms she'd experienced on that day.

One thing was sure…sweat wouldn't wash any better out of her Chanel suit *now* than it had out of Dior *then*.

"Tabby?"

Her sister finally met her stare, appearing almost defiant. "It's simple, really."

The twitching intensified. The moisture on her palms could water the office plants for a week. "Oh?"

"Yes. She can't cheat on our father with the guy if somebody outbids her." With a smile that showed off the twenty-thousand-dollar smile their father had bestowed upon his oldest daughter, Tabitha continued.

"*You* buy the gigolo."

PARAMEDIC JAKE WALLACE had faced death dozens of times since he'd started working with Chicago FD's 4th Battalion five years ago. He'd responded to fires and shootings, to brawls and domestic abuse calls. To riots and hostage standoffs. He'd treated heart attacks, drowning victims and people two steps past death who'd miraculously taken three steps back into existence.

He'd once talked a whacked-out druggie into letting him take his injured girlfriend—whom said druggie had stabbed—out of their house for emergency treatment. And he'd then gotten chewed out by his lieutenant for not following protocol by waiting for the Chicago P.D. to handle it. Right—as if he was going to let her die.

None of those situations had intimidated him.

But this? This scared the hell out of him.

"Why did I ever agree to get involved with this?" he muttered.

One reason. Because he owed his lieutenant big and his lieutenant owed the chief big and the chief's wife loved this particular pet charity. End of story. Which was why two of his buddies from the battalion had already taken their turns under the spotlight.

"I've been asking myself the same thing," a stranger's voice replied.

Jake tugged helplessly at the bow tie that was choking him and glanced at Bachelor Number Eighteen, the one right before *him*. The other man looked just about as happy to be here as Jake, which was saying a lot. Because Jake would just as soon give CPR to a toothless octogenarian with halitosis than stand up on stage and be bid on by a bunch of rich, horny women with way too much time on their hands and too little self-respect. Or self-control.

"I *should* feel better about it," he said, trying to convince himself more than the other final few "bachelors" waiting for their turn on the block. "It is for a good cause, right? So I suffer a few minutes' embarrassment and a bad date. It's worth it."

Number Twenty offered a jaded smile as he leaned indolently against a column in the backstage area that had been set up for this evening's event. The guy looked almost bored, and Jake envied him his calm. "What, you don't enjoy having women 'paying' for your services?" The voice held amusement, and a hint of a foreign accent, possibly Irish.

Maybe European dudes were more at ease playing meat-on-parade. But this all-American rescue worker most definitely was not. "You *do*?"

Number twenty smiled as he checked his sleeves, the gold sheen of expensive cuff links flashing beneath the obviously pricey, tailored tux. Jake would lay money it was not rented.

"It can be…entertaining." This guy's suit and demeanor said he had money enough to donate to worthy causes on his own. But the longish hair scooped back into a black ponytail said he also liked to live dangerously.

So did Jake. But he got quite enough thrills out of putting his ass on the line at emergency scenes, thank you very much. He didn't particularly want to put it out there to be appraised, pinched, ogled or catcalled over by a bunch of strange women with itches between their legs and enough dollar bills to scratch them.

The other man continued. "Besides, as you said, it's for a good cause."

Right. Good cause. Kids. I like kids. Don't have any, don't really want any for a few more years, but they're cute in a long-distance way. As long as they're not sticking raisins up their noses or falling down into sewer drains or following the family cat up a tree.

Okay, so maybe he didn't like kids so much. Not enough to go through this humiliation.

Then he thought about his own baby niece and twin nephews. There was nothing he wouldn't do to make sure they remained the safe, healthy munchkins they were.

Damn. He was going to have to go through with it.

Tugging again at the too-tight collar of his own rent-a-tux, Jake peered through a crease in the black cloth curtains, eyeing the audience. The elegant ballroom was packed with round, white-draped tables, around which sat dozens of women in gowns and shimmery cocktail dresses. Laughter and gossip reigned supreme as they tossed back fruity Cosmos or sparkling champagne. They all watched hungrily, calling out bawdy suggestions as the raucous bidding continued for Bachelor Seventeen, who was currently center stage.

Well, all except one. A brunette who stood about ten feet away from the curtain he was peeking through. She drew his eye as he scanned the crowd…then drew it again. And this time, he let his gaze linger.

She was almost shadowed by one of the giant standing spotlights, which cast gaudy, unforgiving pools of light on the spectacle occurring on the stage. But what he saw of her was definitely enough to pique his interest.

First because she had some wicked curves. She wasn't a tall stick figure in a little black dress like half the women here. Instead she was petite, very rounded with the kind of full curves—generous hips and lush breasts revealed in a low-cut, silky blue dress—that weren't currently fashionable but made his heart pick up its pace and his recently dormant cock come awake in his pants.

Nor did she have bottled blond hair swept up in a complicated hairdo like the other half of the audience. No, hers was dark and thick, with long curls that fell in disarray past her shoulders. The look was wildly seductive, as if she'd just left her bed rather than an exclusive Michigan Avenue beauty salon.

Earthy, sultry, not at all restrained. The woman was sexy in a way that women didn't seem to *allow* themselves to be sexy anymore.

Her looks, however, merely started the fire in his gut. Her untouchable, out-of-place demeanor stoked it until it almost engulfed him.

The brunette wasn't laughing it up with her rich gal pals, or tossing back Manhattans while turning her hand to make sure her diamond rings showed to their greatest flashy advantage. In fact, if he had to guess, he'd say she looked almost disapproving, even tense. He couldn't see her face very well, though he got a glimpse of a stiff little jaw, lifted up in visible determination. And her back was military straight.

He sensed she was keeping it that way intentionally, as if she didn't dare let her guard down lest she be distracted from whatever mission she'd set for herself.

As if realizing she was being watched, the woman glanced around, turning her head enough to cast her face in a bit of light spilling off the stage. Enough to highlight the creamy skin, the curve of her cheek, the fullness of her lips and the dark flash of her eyes.

Beautiful.

Jake's hands clenched into fists at his sides. Though she couldn't possibly see him and was in no way mirroring his reaction, hers did the same.

She clenched out of visible concentration that seemed to swirl around her, creating a no-fly zone between her and everyone else in the room.

He clenched out of pure lust.

He hadn't had sex in a while—not since breaking up with a woman he'd been dating last winter. And nobody had as much as given him a quickened pulse rate since. Not the women he met at the station. Not the ones he helped. Not the nurses at the hospital. Not the hot girl who'd moved in upstairs from him, the one who'd already locked herself out three times just so she'd have an excuse to ask for his help.

This stranger? She'd given him a hard-on from ten feet away.

She looked around the room again, watchful, her gaze passing without hesitation over the crease in the drapes behind which he stood.

Buy me.

She couldn't possibly have heard the mental order, yet she narrowed her eyes, focusing again on the drapes concealing him.

He couldn't help repeating the silent appeal, trying to remember all the stuff one of his sisters had said about that dumb book she'd been obsessed with lately. About how the universe would grant you what you want if you just visualized it hard enough.

Oh, it was easy to come up with some fast-and-hot visualizations right now.

"You want to know my biggest fear?" said Number Eighteen, a blond-haired surfer-looking guy who said he worked as a stockbroker. "What if whoever wins me pays like fifty bucks? I mean, how frigging humiliating would that be when the richest women in Chicago are all drooling like a pack of stray dogs eyeing a butcher shop window out there?"

Mr. Polished European guy laughed softly at the very thought of that even being a possibility for him. Jake, however, immediately understood the stockbroker's worries.

Geez. He'd thought being bid on would be a humiliation. But not being bid on? "Get me out of here."

"Too late," said a perky voice belonging to the young woman who was stage-managing tonight's events. She glanced at the blond pretty boy. "You're on. They're reading the introduction right now." Then she pointed the tip of her pencil at Jake. "And you're right behind him, Nineteen."

Nineteen. That's how they'd addressed him from the moment he'd checked in at the event desk and had been whisked to a private dressing room with all the other saps whose bosses, friends, siblings, mothers or coworkers had talked them into doing this.

Jake glanced through the slit in the drapes again, whispering, "Nineteen."

He could easily envision nineteen things he'd say to the brunette when they met. Nineteen ways to bring about that meeting. The nineteen minutes it would take to run out from behind the curtain, grab her hand and drag her to his place. The number of times he wanted to make love to her and the number of positions he wanted to do it.

"Nineteen? Hello?"

Jake jerked his attention back toward the stage manager who was watching him with an expectant—yet slightly exasperated—look. He'd obviously been visualizing for several minutes. "The guy before you is done."

"What'd he go for?" Jake couldn't help asking.

"Thirty-five."

Thirty-five. Oh, God, thirty-five bucks? He'd whip out his checkbook and pay ten times that if he could get out of this. Then he'd go straight out and introduce himself to the brunette in blue.

"Thirty-five *hundred*," the woman added, obviously reading his expression.

"Holy shit."

He could barely scrape up *one* times that amount, and if he had ten times it in his checking account, he sure as hell wouldn't be living in a one-bedroom apartment over a flower shop in Hyde Park.

"They're reading your bio right now, so we need to move quickly," Miss Pencil Tapper said, actually reaching out to grasp his arm. She must know he wanted to bolt. He doubted he was the first to feel that way tonight.

"Fine, fine," he muttered, not even listening to the announcer, whose voice was droning through the hotel sound system. He let go of the black drape curtain, regret making his fingers glide against it for a moment longer than necessary. Then he was being pushed onto the stage, blinded by a spotlight, deafened by the roar of a hundred tipsy women.

This must be what those Chippendales dudes felt like. The thought of doing this dressed in leather cowboy chaps and nothing else was enough to make his stomach heave.

"Who's going to start the bidding?"

"Five hundred!" someone yelled.

Okay. It was a start. Five hundred…that was a worthy donation. That'd buy a lot of Christmas presents for needy kids. Like, you know, a hundred games of Go Fish or whatever that crap sold for now. But, man, it sounded pathetic considering the pretty boy stockbroker went for seven times that much.

"Six."

"Seven!"

The numbers started flying at a dizzying speed, and Jake couldn't keep up with them for a while. Not until a loud, determined female voice cut through the catcalls to shout, "Five thousand dollars!"

Everyone fell silent for an infinitesimal moment. Jake included. He didn't know what the highest bachelor had sold for, but at least he wasn't going to be rock bottom.

"We have a bid of five thousand dollars for this excellent cause," the auctioneer preened. "And I imagine our handsome bachelor will be worth every penny of it."

Ahh, the joy of being pimped by a fat guy with sweaty jowls and a smarmy smile.

The searing heat of the spotlight suddenly left his face. Jake watched as the large, golden circle washed over the crowd, turning to illuminate the woman who'd ignored auction protocol by upping the ante so dramatically.

Jake held his breath, something in his brain telling him it had been her. The brunette. The one he couldn't stop thinking about had heard his mental 911 call.

The spotlight finally came to rest on the top of a very blond head.

Shit.

The middle-aged woman trying to look ten years younger sat at one of the exclusive, reserved tables up front, with a few other equally jaded-looking upper crusters. She smiled, well pleased with herself for having silenced the entire room.

But the complacent silence didn't last for long. Because suddenly, as if they all had one voice, her three companions jumped into the fray.

"Fifty-one hundred."

"Fifty-two."

"Fifty-five."

It went on for at least a minute, until Jake's head was spinning. These crazy rich females were willing to lay out what amounted to a down payment on a house to go to dinner and a ball game with him? Insane.

It's for a good cause. True, but damned if he wasn't getting tired of hearing that refrain in his head.

The figure had hit eight thousand, the blonde and her three friends laughing as they tossed it higher and higher like a volleyball being lobbed over a net. Jake had hated volleyball ever since he'd been an oversize, clumsy fourth grader who always got picked last for the team in gym. And he especially hated *being* the ball.

Though the bidding women were laughing, their amusement held a hint of malice and their smiles were tight. They might have started this as a game, but now their competitive spirits were rising.

He didn't know how long it might have gone on, if he'd continued to be nibbled at in one-hundred dollar bites. Suddenly the whole room froze again. Because another voice—from the other side of the ballroom—shouted, silencing the three bidding crows.

"Twenty-five thousand dollars."

Jake visualized it, asked the Fates to be kind, then followed the spotlight.

And for once, he realized, his loopy kid sister was right. He'd asked, and the universe had answered. Because the winning bidder was his beautiful brunette.

2

"HOW SHOULD THE CHECK be made out?"

Her pen perched above her open checkbook, Maddy lifted an expectant brow, having finally reached the front of the checkout line for tonight's auction. It was her bad luck that her bachelor had been second to last in the event. If he'd been one of the earlier "prizes," she would have been able to pay the fee and escape early, without running the risk that she'd actually have to face her legally purchased slab of beefcake.

That was the last thing she wanted. She'd done what she'd set out to do—what Tabitha had guilted her into doing. She'd stopped her stepmother from hooking up with another man, at least for tonight. And, at least, with that particular man.

Judging by the look on her stepmother's face, she'd had absolutely no idea any of her husband's family members had been in the audience. When she'd seen Maddy from across the crowded room, Deborah Turner had paled, her eyes had widened in shocked guilt, and she'd rushed out, her nasty, troublemaking best friend Bitsy close behind her.

Too bad Maddy hadn't been outbid at that point. She could have saved herself twenty-five thousand dollars. Because, while she hadn't dated in a while, she most certainly was not desperate enough to actually take advantage of the "prize" she'd just won. If he'd been a regular bachelor? Perhaps. But knowing he was a gigolo who prostituted himself? *Never.*

It's for a good cause, she reminded herself, knowing her family's charitable foundation, which she managed, always supported the worthy children's program anyway.

"I am in a bit of a hurry," she prodded, offering the harried-looking woman running the payment desk a smile to take any sting from her words. "This really is a wonderful program and I'm so glad to be able to support it," she added, meaning it. "But I do have another engagement."

That wasn't exactly untrue. She did have a standing engagement with her remote control and the latest disc from her *Grey's Anatomy* Season 2 DVD set. Better that than sticking around and actually having to converse with a man who accepted money from bored, lonely, rich women.

"You won bachelor number…"

"Nineteen," Maddy supplied, not likely to forget him anytime soon. Oh, she might have no respect for the man, especially because her stepmother had wanted to cheat with him. But he was so damned gorgeous. Even his photograph in the auction program hadn't prepared her to see him in the flesh.

She'd been expecting some kind of skinny, pasty, girlie kind of man like the character in *American Gigolo*. She had not imagined anything like those shoulders, which were about the width of a small bus, or the bulked-up chest straining against the fabric of his tux. Nor the thick dark hair, cut short enough to tempt a woman to do some finger tangling while not drawing one bit of attention away from the slashing brows, the prominent cheekbones, the stubborn chin.

He was all man. Nothing like what she'd expected. Although, she had to admit, her ideas *had* been based on movie references and her own interactions with weaker-willed men who used women. *Don't even go there*, a voice in her head reminded her.

"You can make the check out to Give A Kid A Christmas," the attractive, dark-haired woman behind the counter said. She offered Maddy a grateful smile. "And thank you so much. Yours was the most generous donation of the night."

"I'm sure it'll be put to good use."

"Absolutely," the woman said. She gestured toward the nearest door. "By the way, we've set up a private reception down the hall, for our winning bidders and our bachelors to meet. You know, to break the ice before any private, um…meetings."

Assignations was more like it.

Addressing the check, Maddy merely smiled politely, not replying. Then, giving the woman her payment and taking a tax receipt in return, she deliberately swung around and walked in the opposite direction.

She'd done her job. Now she needed to get out of here. She'd come in late—having been tipped off by Tabitha that her target would be auctioned off second to last. She hadn't seen anyone she knew, other than her stepmother and the woman's friends. Hopefully, she could escape without any further public exposure of her foray into the flesh trade.

She almost made it. She was mere feet from the closest ballroom exit when she was stopped by a movable wall disguised as a tuxedo shirt.

Her heart leaped in her chest, thudding in excitement, even as she mentally cursed the bad luck. Because Number Nineteen had tracked her down.

"Hello," the wall murmured. "I'm Jake Wallace."

Maddy growled a little, annoyed at herself for feeling an immediate tingle at the warmth emanating off the solid man now blocking her path. And for leaning forward the tiniest bit and breathing a bit deeper to catch a better whiff of his warm, spicy scent.

"I know we're supposed to be meeting in the reception room," he added, "but I'd rather head to the hotel bar, too, if that's where you were going. I don't think I could stand another hour with that crowd."

Funny that he already knew, somehow, that Maddy was not of "that crowd." Oh, she fit in financially, *and* she had the family connections and pedigree to mix with the best of Chicago society. But she didn't like them, didn't feel comfortable with them, preferring to listen to Tabitha's cutting first-person reports rather than experience the flighty world of the rich-and-shameless personally. Her social interactions usually centered around business—fund-raisers, executive dinners. Certainly not hot-body auctions.

"That is where you were going, right? You weren't trying to ditch me." It wasn't a question and his tone held a hint of laughter. She didn't think his amusement was caused by conceit, but rather the incongruity of a woman paying twenty-five thousand dollars to spend an evening with a man and then walking out the door without ever meeting him.

It *was* kind of crazy.

"I, uh…the ladies' room," she mumbled, hating herself for letting the inane excuse cross her lips the very moment she uttered it. Ladies' room indeed. Deborah, her socially impeccable—if potentially adulterous—stepmother, would be flaring her nostrils in mortification. *If* she wasn't cowering somewhere, wondering if Maddy was going to rat her out for trying to buy her way into this man's arms.

He cleared his throat. "It's that way."

His arm moved, the hand gesturing back the way Maddy had just come. That hand was darkly tanned, strong, with neat blunt fingernails and not a hint of kept-man elegance. They looked like a worker's hands. And suddenly several parts of Maddy's body went a little spastic at the thought of being *worked* by them.

Not being the tallest woman in the world, Maddy had been able to keep her attention squarely focused straight ahead, as if minutely interested in the design of the buttons on his shirt. Since she'd been sucked in by his hands, though, she figured she might as well muster up the courage to confront the rest of him.

She could do it. She was woman. Hear her roar.

All she could manage as she lifted her gaze, however, was a helpless whimper.

The chest was, as she already knew, huge and strong. The throat tanned, the neck corded with muscle. His strong jaw jutted in classic male determination. His face was freshly shaved, she'd imagined, for tonight's event, but already displayed a hint of swarthiness that would provide the tiniest frisson of roughness if their cheeks met.

They won't.

Even if she acknowledged how physically attractive he was, she still would never again take up with a man who couldn't keep his pants zipped. She'd been down that road before.

Still…he *was* handsome. His thick hair was cut short, and had looked lighter when he was up on stage, being paraded around like a prime bit of horseflesh for sale. Now, up close, she realized it was a dark brown, but shot with hints of gold here and there that said he likely spent a lot of time outside. Probably sailing around in yachts owned by rich women, hitting the clubs in Monaco or cruising the Mediterranean. Doing the types of things people in her social circle took for granted, too.

None of which interested *her.*

Except, maybe, lounging under the sun on a clear blue sea. She might not like the ennui and shallowness that often came with extreme wealth, but she wasn't stupid. She enjoyed an occasional luxury as much as the next silver spoon girl. And a summer day spent sailing on her father's thirty-three-foot cutter was one of her few genuine indulgences.

"Why don't you let me escort you?" he added, finally breaking the silence.

"I'm afraid I was just leaving," she admitted, knowing she needed to end this now, before he offered to lead her to the closest ladies' room. Maybe even escort her inside…and do her in the lavish vestibule.

Oh, God, what a fantasy.

She cleared her throat. "It's a work night."

Finally allowing herself to meet his gaze directly, all remaining words dried up in Maddy's mouth. Because those eyes, which she hadn't been able to see clearly from the audience, were a dark, warm brown, so friendly and approachable, open and engaging that it was impossible to imagine this man was anything but an all-American boy-next-door. Albeit the handsomest one she'd ever met.

There was merriment in those eyes, and warmth and friendliness. Not jaded awareness, not arrogance. Just…niceness. And pure laid-back sex appeal.

That didn't fit what she knew about the man. Not one bit.

"Work?" he asked, sounding as though he'd never heard the word.

Well, maybe he hadn't. Maddy lifted her chin, ignoring those eyes, that half smile on his sensual mouth, and forced herself to remember who this brown-eyed, kind-looking hottie really was.

A man for sale.

"Yes. Work," she snapped. "I came here to support a charity. I've done it, and now I'm leaving."

He put a hand out, touching her elbow lightly, though not trying to restrain her. But all the same, the touch was binding, rooting her where she stood.

"Look, I have the feeling we've gotten off on the wrong foot somehow. I'd really like to go sit down somewhere, not as part of our 'date' but just so I can thank you for bidding on me." He shook his head, smiled slightly and rubbed a hand across his strong jaw, the slide of his fingers rasping the tiniest bit across his very faint five-o'clock shadow. "You saved me from being the cheapest guy of the night."

"As if that was going to happen."

"You never know. That stockbroker guy was offering a weekend getaway upstate."

"What were you offering?" she asked, only out of curiosity. *Not* out of genuine interest. Definitely not.

Shrugging, he admitted, "A home game at Wrigley Field followed by wings and beer at a pub."

Maddy's eyebrows went up.

"You didn't know that when you shelled out twenty-five thousand bucks?"

She shook her head, muttering, "I don't think it would have mattered."

Not one bit. Because neither Bitsy Wellington, or Maddy's stepmother would ever have let that ball game evening happen. The date would have begun and ended tonight, right in one of the thousand lavish hotel rooms above their heads. Despite being much older than this man, Deborah had the money, the looks and the charm to make sure she got exactly what she wanted. Whether Jake Wallace had really intended a "normal" date with the winner or not.

To Maddy, though, a Major League ball game sounded wonderful. She'd never been to a professional game, relying on ESPN and pay-per-view channels to satisfy her innate—if secret, given its less-than-spoiled-little-rich-girl image—love of sports. Especially sports that took place on a diamond and involved a bat and a ball.

So borrow Dad's box seats. Because you aren't *going with Mr. Expensive.*

"You see why I was expecting the worst. I mean, if somebody had gotten me for twenty bucks, my sisters would never have let me hear the end of it."

She couldn't prevent a trill of amused laughter from escaping her lips at the very thought of this man getting out of here for such a paltry amount. He probably charged that much per minute.

He watched her laugh, those soft, dreamy eyes resting on her lips, his own curling up at the edges in response. "You've got dimples."

She clamped her lips tight, silently ordering her cheeks to flatten out.

"They're beautiful."

"They're stupid."

"Adorable."

"Made for a five-year-old's face or a baby's bottom."

He shook his head. "Uh-uh. A beautiful woman's."

Maddy quivered at that. Though she knew the man was probably schooled at such come-ons, and made a practice of making every woman feel beautiful and desirable, she couldn't help the warm flow of pleasure surging through her veins. Because he made her *believe* it.

His lips quirked. "Uh, by that I meant a beautiful woman's *face*, of course."

Remembering the second part of her comment, she inwardly groaned, mortified at having given the man such an easy opening.

"You really are stunning," he murmured, not handing her a line, not at all sleazy. Just confident of what he said. "A dark and vibrant flame next to all those icy princesses."

Maddy swallowed. It wasn't possible that he *knew* her—and her reputation—was it? No. He couldn't. He was using his wiles, his tricks of the trade, telling her what he thought she wanted to hear, like any good professional. Because far from being the vibrant "flame," she was known as the coldest businesswoman in Chicago.

Did he really see her so differently?

"You looked entirely *alive* from up on that stage…the only woman who did."

Okay, boy-next-door or not, the man was good at getting around a woman's defenses with that sexy-smooth delivery. Too good. Especially since she knew there was no way she could have him. Just the thought of what might have happened between him and her stepmother had she not prevented it was enough to make her stomach turn.

Besides, never again would she be with someone who had sex with more partners in a month than she'd had in her lifetime. Been there, done that. Her ex simply had not gotten paid for it. He hadn't needed to. He'd quite enjoyed giving it away for free to any woman who'd spread her legs.

Well…she had to give this Jake some credit. At least he was honest and open about what he was.

That, however, was as much as she was willing to concede. "I have to go."

"Oh, come on," he urged, "please don't. You've got to at least let me buy you a beer for saving me from utter humiliation in front of that bloodthirsty crowd."

"And from your sisters."

"Who are absolutely merciless."

His tone said he didn't care, that there was a genuine fondness between him and his siblings. Well, Maddy understood that. Though she might have little to nothing in common with Tabby, that didn't mean she didn't love her. She understood the concept of loving someone even if you didn't completely understand them. If not, she'd never have survived this many years in her own family.

"I have one of those."

"Sisters?"

She nodded. "And she's also pretty merciless. Especially about getting her own way."

"I somehow suspect you can hold your own."

"Ditto."

"I always found that hanging their bras out their bedroom windows was an effective deterrent to future harassment."

Maddy couldn't help chuckling again, unable to keep a smile off her face, dimple exposure or not. "I don't know that Tabitha's ever owned one," she replied, thinking of her sister's willowy, graceful figure. Tabby was Gwyneth Paltrow slender all the way. While Maddy was more on the Catherine Zeta Jones side.

He glanced down, probably not even aware he was doing it. The glance was quick, not offensive, probably almost reflex considering the need to check out a woman's breasts seemed inbred into male genes.

His gaze rose to her face, but not so quickly that she didn't see the way his jaw flexed and his eyes narrowed, shining with dark intensity and appreciation, all traces of that easygoing good humor disappearing.

Hers disappeared, as well. Not to be replaced by anger…but by pure physical awareness. The roam of his stare over her body affected her just as thoroughly as a real touch from anyone else would have.

Sometimes, she didn't mind so much being the more curvaceous of the Turner sisters. Tabitha had the runway model shape and maintained it by eating as much as a three-day-old sparrow. Maddy, meanwhile, bordered on voluptuous, from her more than ample breasts to her small waist and downright generous hips, and fought every potato chip and cheesecake urge to keep it that way.

Her body might play hell with her wardrobe, ruling out any cute little backless sundress or strapless gowns, which Tabby had by the roomful. But right now, at this moment, she couldn't bring herself to care. And it was all because of the heat in this sexy man's eyes and the almost audible quality of his next, slowly indrawn breath.

That was lust she saw there. Pure and undisguised, unhidden by social demands or proper breeding that insisted it wasn't polite to visibly covet a woman.

He was coveting. She was being coveted. They were both caught in the tension of it.

Though her mind knew better, her body couldn't help responding. Beneath the silky dress, her skin puckered, tiny goose bumps rising on the deep V of her cleavage, her nipples tightening to jut against the lace of her bra. Her pulse fluttered in her throat, and the breaths she managed to inhale were shallow. Each was filled with the warmth of him and the dark, masculine scent of his body, which had edged to within inches of her own.

All from a look. What in God's name might happen to her if he ever laid a hand on her?

"Please say yes," he murmured. "For no other reason than that you want to."

His tone remained light, not demanding, not intense, despite the look in his eyes and the static in the air between them. As if he knew that coming on too strong might scare her off.

And suddenly, it was working. Her verbal defenses had been firmly in place at the start, but now…well, now she'd actually allowed herself to see him as a person—a very sexy person— rather than just the instrument her stepmother had intended to use to hurt her father.

If he'd played the lothario, Maddy would already have been out of here. But he hadn't. He'd merely sounded friendly, engaging, and oh *so* tempting. While he spoke of polite things like his family, his eyes did all the more intimate talking. He *wanted* her, yet managed to remain genuine and self-deprecating. Not at all like the male prostitute he was.

Suddenly remembering what else Tabby had told her about the man, and the glimpse she'd had at the auction program, she said, "You don't have an accent!"

"Am I supposed to?"

She clenched her lips shut, wishing she'd thought to learn a bit more about what she was up against tonight. Tabitha had given her the bare bones and Maddy had raced into the plan. Typical story. Just the way it was when they were kids and Tabby had been Lucy holding the ball while Charlie Brown Maddy ran down the field to kick it, *knowing* she was going to end up on her ass.

"I should have made her do it herself," Maddy muttered,

though she knew that would have been a very bad idea. Even Tabitha had known better.

Maddy could be trusted to avoid a sexy gigolo. Hopefully. Her sister could not. And Tabby seemed truly determined to make her next marriage—which was scheduled for its high society kickoff in a few weeks—work. She would *never* have been able to keep her perfectly manicured fingers off this hunk.

But Maddy could. And she would. Any moment now. As soon as her heart slowed down and her body came off orange alert and went back down to at least yellow.

"What?"

"Nothing." Maddy stared at him, searching for something in his expression, a hint that a predator lurked beneath his oh-so-sexy, laid-back, nice-guy appearance. There must be something—malice, greed, or lasciviousness—behind the open, honest interest in his stare. Just because she hadn't seen it, didn't mean it wasn't there.

There *had* to be more to him than she was seeing. And she almost wished she had time to find it.

Maybe if she'd been introduced to him at a cocktail party or met him at the bank, she'd allow herself to fall for the sexy, charming, friendly demeanor and let herself be seduced by the want in his eyes. She would try to get to know him better, and let him know his physical interest was most definitely reciprocated.

But one undeniable truth prevented that.

If she had not been tipped off and come here tonight to prevent it, the man standing in front of her would probably be upstairs having sex with her father's wife right this minute.

And that was the end of her waffling. Again repulsed by the very idea, Maddy took a step away, removing her arm from his touch, and the rest of her from the force field of sexiness encompassing the man like a cloak. She was immune, damn it. Mentally and, now, because of the harsh truth she'd just forced herself to acknowledge, physically.

Maddy pasted the cordial but not exactly friendly, expression on her face she used daily when running interference between her father and the sycophants constantly hitting him up. "Really, Mr. Wallace, there's no wrong foot. You don't owe me a thing. I'm glad I was able to keep you from the ridicule of your sisters." With a deliberately rueful smile, she thought of how she'd ended up here tonight and admitted, "They can definitely be annoying."

"Okay then. So we'll have a drink while we compare our crazy families, make our plans and check out the sports page for the next home game." Frowning, he added, "You *are* a Cubs fan, aren't you?"

"I think it's illegal not to be around here."

"Meaning there's nothing stopping us from going out."

"If I told you I liked the Cardinals, would that get this ridiculous idea out of your head?" He lifted a hand to his chest, his jaw opening in horror. Which made her laugh again. "Kidding."

"You'd go that far to avoid going out with me?" he asked, his voice growing quiet, his smile fading. As if her answer really mattered to him…as if he *cared*.

Shaking her head, Maddy stepped around him, taking that first all-important step toward the door. And away from Mr. Superstud. "It's not about going out with you. I had my own reasons for being here tonight, and they didn't include a date. So you are completely off the hook."

"But the money…"

"Was for the children." *And for my father.* "There's no quid pro quo in this." Even if five minutes ago all her most feminine parts had been demanding that she get at least a little bit of quid and a whole lot of quo for being so…*awakened* by him.

That was a good word for it. Their brief conversation hadn't aroused her quite to the level of blatant physical desire. But it had most definitely awakened her to the possibilities. Especially because she suddenly realized that as well as being physically attracted to him, she could also truly like this warm, amusing man.

Oh, there were *so* many possibilities.

No. They were *im*possibilities. Her most feminine parts would have to be happy watching hot doctors having affairs at Seattle Grace.

Telling herself she would not regret this in the morning, but wondering how she'd make it through the long, lonely night ahead without fantasizing about how she *could* have spent it— she murmured "Goodbye," and walked out of his life.

JAKE HAD THREE SISTERS, so he knew better than to try to change a woman's mind when she had definitely made it up. And the sexy brunette in the silky blue dress had most assuredly made up her mind to leave. Funny, though…he had the feeling she'd decided to ditch him before she'd ever bid on him.

Which, frankly, made him feel a lot better. Because her disinterest was not personal. He just needed to make sure that her *interest* became *very* personal.

Because there was no way that pert little dismissal and the sashay of her curvy hips out the ballroom door was the end of their relationship. Uh-uh. She'd been sexy and mysterious, aloof and unattainable from behind that black curtain. Now that he'd seen those stormy brown eyes, heard that whiskey-toned voice and caught a glimpse of her beautiful smile and those adorable dimples, he found her not only sexy and earthy but also almost heart-stoppingly desirable.

And no longer unattainable. He had a legitimate reason to find her. A good reason. He owed her what he'd promised and he never welshed on a deal.

Jake didn't even consider following her. He didn't need to. Chicago might be a big city, but the world in which the über-wealthy lived was a small, incestuous one. He could find out who she was with a few well-placed questions at the reception going on down the hall.

The problem was, he really didn't want to venture into that reception. He'd escaped the clutches of the catcalling rich bitches and he had no desire to fall into them again. Fortunately, he didn't have to.

"Excuse me," he said as he strode toward the checkout desk. It was almost deserted now, with just a few last volunteers counting cash, sorting checks and cleaning up after the flesh-spending-frenzy.

"Yes?" an attractive brunette replied. Jake recognized her as the woman who ran the charity organization benefiting from tonight's auction—the Give A Kid A Christmas thing that provided traditional holiday seasons for families living in Chicago's abused women shelters. Noelle something. She'd been earnest and friendly, a little harried, but not coolly amused and assessing the way some of the auction organizers had been when he'd arrived.

"I must be brain-dead," he said, offering her a smile. "But I somehow let the woman who won the date with me get away without making our final plans. And I don't know how to get in touch with her."

The woman frowned. "What was her name?"

Sticky one. Jake thought about bullshitting some more, then decided honesty was probably the best way to go. If the brunette felt sorry for him at having been bought and then dumped like yesterday's garbage, she might be more forthcoming with the information he wanted.

"To be honest? She didn't give it to me. I think she got cold feet, even after laying out twenty-five grand."

Recognition washed over the woman's face. "Ah, yes, I remember her." As if wanting to console him, she added, "She did say she had to be somewhere else. I'm sure she was in a hurry and didn't realize she hadn't given you her name and number."

"That must have been it. I'd really appreciate your help, uh…Noelle, right?"

"Right," she replied. "Noelle Santori." Turning her attention toward the money she'd been counting, she added, "She won't be hard to find. There was only one check made out in that amount tonight."

The woman riffled through a stack of checks piled inside the metal strongbox, plucked one out and said, "Aha!" Then she frowned. "Uh-oh, it's a foundation, not a personal check. Her name's not printed on here, and her signature is a little…messy."

"Her name is Madeline Turner," a woman behind him said. Jake swung around and saw a slender, attractive blonde, watching him with hooded speculation. He didn't know her, as far as he could tell. She might have been one of the horny, diamond-laden princesses bidding fast and hard during the auction. Or she might not. The spotlights hadn't allowed him a close enough look to be certain.

"Here," the blonde said, handing him a business card. "Maddy works at a bank downtown. That's the address." She gave him a thorough once-over, assessing him as if he was a six-foot-three lobster in a fancy restaurant's tank. And she was very hungry for some surf and turf.

Finally, she sighed and crossed her arms. "I'm sure it was an oversight, her leaving without getting what she came here for. So you be sure to look her up." She turned away, tugging her weather-inappropriate stole tighter around her shoulders. As she walked away, he caught one final whisper. "You might just be an answer to a prayer."

3

"EXCUSE ME, MISS TURNER, there's someone to see you."

Madeline looked up from her desk as her administrative assistant, Ella, peeked around the partially open door to her office. Being addressed as Miss Turner tipped her off to her young employee's unusually somber mood. Most times, the efficient-but-bubbly young woman would have buzzed her, reminded her of an appointment, then snapped a quick, naughty joke. Ella liked nothing better than leaving Madeline with an inappropriate grin on her face as some staid business visitor entered her office.

This time, though, Ella sounded subdued, almost awed, and wore a facial expression to match.

"Oh, damn, is it the congressman again? I told him we weren't increasing his line of credit."

The other woman shook her head slowly. "Nope. A stranger." Clearing her throat, she blinked a few times, as if trying to physically shake off her dazed mood. After a few seconds, she grinned. And when she began speaking in a rush, Maddy realized her *real* assistant was back in the building.

"Look, I just have to say, if this is a sales guy running a scam and he doesn't *really* know you and doesn't *really* have an appointment, I will so totally take him off your hands. I'll whisk him out of here, no problem. Show him the door, follow him out, go somewhere private and whip him into shape. Give him a good, stern talking-to about coming by without appointments." Her expression verging between lustful and hopeful, she added, "It would probably take hours and hours. Maybe the whole weekend."

Ella wasn't exactly the most professional bank employee in the world, but she was by no means flighty. Which meant whoever Maddy's visitor was, he had to be someone capable of turning a normal, levelheaded young woman into a jazzed-up, sexed-up, babbling twit.

"Oh, hell," she whispered, knowing who was standing right outside her door. Only one man she'd met recently was capable of sucking every brain cell from a woman's head within two minutes of meeting her.

Considering she'd dreamed about him for the past two nights—hot, *Grey's Anatomy* inspired dreams of her being the filling in a triple decker McSteamy, McDreamy and McGigolo sandwich—she should be feeling McPanicked and McCornered. He'd almost surely be able to read the guilty embarrassment on her face the moment he spotted her.

Somehow, though, she could only muster anticipation and excitement. But she knew that all he'd see on her face was interest and admiration that he'd tracked her down—and sought her out—so quickly.

"Show him in," she murmured, knowing she had about thirty seconds, the time it would take Ella to walk out and Number Nineteen to walk in. Just enough time to touch her hair, smooth her blouse and cross her legs.

She uncrossed them and slid her chair under her desk as soon as he entered. Her skirt wasn't *too* short. It was perfectly business-like, in fact. But the pose seemed a little too blatant... inviting. As if she wanted to encourage him sexually, letting him know he'd been all she'd had on her mind since the moment she'd met him.

That she did, and he *was* didn't change her decision to go for professional rather than come-hither.

"Hi," he said. "Found ya."

"So you did, Mr. Wallace."

"Nice to see you again…Miss *Turner.*" He glanced around her cluttered office, at the shelves laden with books and files and the stack of documents awaiting her signature in her in-box. Then he gazed past her at the window overlooking the city, one of the best views in the high-rise building. Whistling, he murmured, "I guess you do have a real job."

"What made you think I didn't?"

He met her stare, saying nothing.

"Okay," she acknowledged with a grudging smile. "I don't suppose many of the bidders from the auction work on much more than their tans."

"But you don't have one. Meaning you obviously work too much."

"It could be that I'm naturally pale-skinned and prone to burning." And that she hadn't had one of those lazy summer days on her father's boat since *last* summer. She was going to have to remedy that.

"I somehow suspect you spend twelve hours a day in here and just wave at the sun from your window as it goes by."

Smart man. And one who was right now making himself at home, sitting in a chair opposite her desk without being asked. Her office almost seemed to shrink around him, as if his big body had sucked up all the spare particles of air, leaving the two of them cloaked tightly in intimacy.

Thank God for the desk. If it hadn't been between them, Maddy might have been tempted to slide her chair closer, until their knees touched. Or their thighs. Or their mouths.

Stop it.

"Why'd you ditch me?"

"Why did you pursue me?"

"Ha. I asked you a complicated question and you asked me

a very simple one." He grinned. "I tracked you down because I owe you a date and I am not a welsher."

That was all. He wasn't a welsher. Well, didn't she just feel special, like an average everyday poker player waiting for a five-dollar payoff.

"Now, your turn."

"It isn't necessarily complicated." She arched a brow and managed a bored tone. "Maybe I ditched you because I wasn't interested."

His grin still confident, he immediately dispelled that possibility. "Twenty-five thousand bucks is a whole lot of disinterest."

"It's for a worthy cause."

"So why didn't you bid on somebody else early in the evening and get out right away?"

"What makes you think I didn't? Maybe you were my second-to-the-last chance to make a difference, so I made an outrageous bid."

"You didn't bid on anybody else." He leaned toward her desk, dropping his elbows on its surface. "Admit it." The position sent muscle surging against cotton as his casual, washed-out T-shirt hugged his arms. The flexing of his tanned skin against the black fabric was almost impossible to tear her gaze away from. She honestly didn't think she'd ever seen a more powerfully built man in person.

She knew she'd never slept with one.

Most of the men Maddy had had sex with had been wiry young college guys who wanted any female they could get—especially wealthy, heiress females—or pale, soft businessmen she met in her usual circle. Those men—men like Oliver, her ex-lover, whom she'd kicked out of her life a year and a half ago—were generally toned from their weekend tennis game or occasional golf tournaments. Or, in Oliver's case, from his frequent ski trips with his "best friend" Roddy.

That Roddy had been a nickname for Rhonda, a twenty-year-old ski bunny, had been something he'd failed to mention. Maddy had found out the hard way when she'd decided to surprise him one weekend. She'd found Oliver in his room, engaging in some serious downhill action with the snow ho.

There were no skis involved, but his pole had been getting quite a workout.

She thrust away the memory, acknowledging that in the several months she'd dated the man, she'd *never* looked at him and immediately lusted the way she did with the guy sitting on the other side of her desk. Jake Wallace had the kind of massive, rock-solid body women dreamed existed but never expected to see in real life.

And she coveted it. As *he'd* been coveting the other night.

"I don't think you bid on anyone else," he murmured, speaking softly, as if aware she'd been struck a little brainless. "I was watching you from behind the curtain for a long time."

Feeling a bubble of air lodge in the center of her throat, Maddy struggled to swallow it down, but couldn't quite manage it.

He had been watching her. Watching. *Her*. With all the tall, elegant, skinny women in the room, *she'd* caught his eye…and had apparently kept it.

In some contexts, hearing a man saying he'd been "watching her" could creep a woman out. But this didn't. Just the way his hungry stare hadn't the night they'd met.

Instead, once again, he appeared so…honest. Open about his feelings. Jake sounded both confident and almost surprised by his own admission, as if he hadn't meant to reveal his immediate interest in her, even though his presence here in her office confirmed it.

He's a pro at making women feel this way, a small voice in her head reminded her.

"I even started asking the universe to let you be the one to win me," he admitted.

Startled into laughter, Maddy knew exactly what he meant. Tabitha had recently been touting the brilliance of the same self-help bestseller. She swore it was the reason she'd landed her latest fiancé, a well-known Chicago hotelier, who was nice, a bit dull, but richer than an oil baron.

"You don't strike me as the type who needs any *secret* when it comes to winning over a woman, Mr. Wallace."

"I obviously needed to find out one secret…your identity."

Smooth.

"Fortunately, like Cinderella, you left a clue behind."

"I think I had both shoes on my feet when I got home."

"Your check. With your signature."

Frowning, she crossed her arms and leaned back in her chair. "They gave you my check?"

"Just a quick peek. Then a helpful stranger told me the rest of what I needed to know."

How *kind* of the stranger.

Honestly, though, considering she was edgy and excited, her pulse a little fast, her heart beating a little hard, maybe it *had* been a kindness. Maddy hadn't dated anyone in a long time. The last scene with her ex had burned itself on her brain and left her skeptical of the sweet promises of *any* man. Oliver's final words—when he'd insisted they could still be a great team with her money and his family connections, with no messy, intimate "emotions" attached—had replayed in her mind many times since then.

She was a suitable candidate for the position of Oliver's wife, with an acceptable pedigree and lots of cash. A great business prospect. Nothing more.

Ouch.

"Everybody knows everybody in your circle, huh?"

"It's the world's biggest small pond."

"Yawn."

"You've no idea."

"So come swim outside the reef with me. You might not be surrounded by your colorful, tropical kind, but sometimes us plain old trout can be entertaining."

Maddy couldn't help chuckling again. The man was just cute. As if he could be plain old *anything*. "You know, lately, I've been sticking to the shallows."

"Double yawn. Come on, take a chance."

Uh-uh. The shallows suited her fine. Here she could safely ignore any thoughts of her personal life. Along with working insane hours, she'd been dealing with the usual family crises, including Tabby's upcoming wedding. The social functions she attended were more a matter of courtesy and professionalism than pleasure and the men she met at them always fell into two camps—the boring and proper, or the greedy, who saw dollar signs on her forehead.

The first type could never catch her interest. The second made her skin crawl. None of them could ever make her consider swimming out into those romance waters again. She just wasn't interested.

Until now.

Yes. Until now. This man had slowed her down, made her think, made her aware of herself for the first time in ages. For that, at least, she owed him thanks. Because though she still had no intention of letting anything happen between her and a paid companion, she had at least begun to wonder if she should accept a few more invitations, get out more and perhaps meet someone else who *could* get her heart tripping and her palms damp. And maybe even her panties.

She'd guard her heart, set out for some physical satisfaction and never let herself be hurt. As long as she went into it with that in mind, it could be possible for her to have some kind of sex life again.

With him.

"No," she whispered. Not with him. Because, while his career might actually be a benefit, given the no-strings, pleasure-only kind of affair she suddenly had in mind, her reaction to him was already way too personal, too strong and intimate for her to feel comfortable. He made her laugh, he made her blush, he made her palms sweat. And she could not be one hundred percent sure his feelings were genuine and not merely evidence of how good he was at what he did.

Ergo, he was out of the question as a potential easy, sex-and-go fling.

"No?" he said, obviously hearing her whisper. "You really mean that?" Before she could say yes, he quickly continued. "Because even if you didn't set out to buy a date and you were only supporting the charity," he said, sounding as though he only half believed that, "I did *not* go into it that way. I agreed to a date and I'm trying to live up to my end of the bargain here."

"Your bargain…"

"I made a promise to the organizers of the auction and my promise is like my handshake. My dad would clobber me if I didn't stand by either one of them. So that's what I am going to do."

Whether you like it or not. He didn't say the words. But she heard them just the same.

Maddy noted the challenge, realized he was throwing down a gauntlet, daring her to *not* live up to her end of the bargain. And her competitive spirit rose. She might have been raised in a mansion, but the owner of that mansion had been Jason Turner, who had his financial hands spread over half the city and his fingers touching the other half. He kept them there by shrewdness and sheer will. Something else she'd inherited from her dad.

She suspected their fathers would get along well.

"All right then," she said, meeting his stare, "so will I."

"You won't regret it," he said, his eyes darkening even further as he stared at her, raking his gaze from her hair to her cheek, then to her mouth and her throat in a look more appreciative than predatory.

She already regretted it. How had she let herself be dared into saying yes?

She opened her mouth to lay down a few ground rules for their "date." It would be brief, platonic and completely romance-free, without question. She fully intended to meet him at the ball field and leave immediately after the last out of the night. And that would be the end of it.

No touching. No sexy looks. None of those cute jokes that made the stupid dimples on her face put in an appearance. And from here on out, her palms were staying dry. So were her private parts.

Before she could say anything, however, they were both startled by the sudden opening of Maddy's office door.

"Maddy, I need to talk to you about…oh, I'm sorry. I didn't know you had an appointment. Your secretary's not outside and your calendar was clear."

Maddy leaped from her seat so quickly her chair went sliding backward against the wall. Her father had just entered the room, carrying a folder and wearing his "We have a problem" look that usually meant they were skipping lunch.

He quickly forgot his problem though, as he stared curiously at Jake Wallace. Maybe because nobody had been on her electronic appointment calendar. Maybe because the dark-haired man was smiling too intimately to be a client looking for a loan. Maybe because Maddy was so flustered. Or maybe because the heated tension in her office was about as thick as the stack of her father's prenups and divorce notices.

Which was pretty damn thick.

"Dad!" she said, wondering how her day could have gone downhill so rapidly. No more words came out of her mouth. Her brain had just emptied, probably because the whole reason she'd attended the bachelor auction was to keep her father's wife out of *this* man's bed.

Jake stood, saving her from having to say anything. But when he spoke, Maddy wondered whether he'd done her any favors at all.

"I'm not an appointment," he said, smiling at her father, comfortable and at ease as he rose to extend his hand. "I'm Madeline's date, and I'm here to take her to lunch."

"I THINK your father likes me."

Jake didn't have to hear the annoyed, huffy little sound Madeline Turner made to know she wasn't happy about that. He could still picture the mortification on her face when her father, the very well-known Jason Turner, had practically pushed her out the door with her lunch "date" after offering Jake a hearty handshake and a broad smile.

Funny, he'd have thought coming face-to-face with one of the wealthiest men in Chicago would have been at least slightly intimidating. Jason Turner might not be known nationwide, but there wasn't a person in Chicago who hadn't heard of the rich philanthropist, a man who was as well-known for his charitable works as for his stormy love life.

Jake hadn't been intimidated, though. Maybe it was because he'd seen enough accident scenes, helped enough crime victims, responded to enough tragedies, that he realized all the money in the world didn't mean a damn thing when it came to stopping a bullet or avoiding flying through the windshield of a car.

Everyone bled the same—red. There was no such thing as blue blood. Which was, perhaps, why he also felt entirely at ease in his pursuit of Madeline Turner, who the society pages liked to call the Ice Queen of the Financial District. He'd found that out in the two days since the auction. He'd been doing some research.

Personally, she wasn't a bit icy. Confident and a little unreachable? Sure. But not cold.

Professionally? Well, he really didn't give a damn what she was like behind that fancy desk at work. He didn't want her for her connections to a major Chicago bank. He wanted her for the excitement he'd felt in his gut from the moment he'd peered at her from behind the black drapes at the auction the other night. And he wanted to know what had been behind her tension and her determination, which hadn't been able to disguise her innate earthy sensuality.

"Don't let it go your head," she said as they reached the corner of Madison and State, heading for the closest lunch café. "Despite his business reputation, my father is a hopeless romantic, who'd love to see me settle down. He'd be happy if an intoxicated mime in full makeup came to take me to lunch, as long as he was single and breathing."

"I hate mimes."

"Who doesn't?"

"I mean, what kind of kid thinks 'Gee, when I grow up, I wanna paint my face and annoy people for a living.'"

She raised a droll brow. "One who wants to be a clown?"

"I think I'd feel better if my kid said he wanted to be a lawyer."

"Perish the thought," she said with an exaggerated shudder.

"I've never seen a drunk one, though. That might be entertaining."

"You obviously don't lunch at the Chicago Club with all the rest of the high-priced defense attorneys."

"I meant the mime," he explained, enjoying sparring with her, liking the smart comebacks and that smile lurking on her mouth.

What he most wanted now was a full frontal attack of those gorgeous dimples and that light laugh he just knew was hiding behind the twitching lips and the twinkling eyes.

"Watching them fall and not be able to get up in their invisible box might be fun."

It finally worked, he got her to relax. "You're right." A tiny grin appeared, finally widening into that brilliant smile, complete with a flash of those dimples. God, she had the kind of smile that could stop traffic. She was absolutely made for it.

Among other things.

Feeling even more confident about his sneaky way of getting her to have lunch with him, he took her arm as the light changed. Instinct. Good manners toward females had been hammered into him from the time he was old enough to understand what the words *put the seat down* meant.

One good thing—she didn't flinch. A second one—she didn't pull away, either. It was something, at least.

"So your dad's a real romantic, huh?" The image didn't quite fit with the "ruthless mogul" the papers made him out to be.

"Don't go there."

"Touchy subject?"

"His romantic track record's not exactly one for the books. Yet he still wants everything to be roses and fairy tales, true love all around, as impossible as that may be."

They crossed the street with the rest of the streaming flow of humanity. On a sunny summer afternoon, *everyone* stepped outside to bask in the sunlight. And many of them did it at Millennium Park. That was where he intended to take Madeline after they grabbed a take-out lunch. He sensed she wasn't the picnicking type, especially in the middle of a workday, but he intended to try to convince her, anyway.

"Why is it impossible?" he asked as they stepped onto the opposite sidewalk.

"What?" she asked, glancing up at him in confusion, obviously having forgotten what she'd just said.

That said a lot. Mainly that she didn't think about love very often. He tucked the realization away, knowing he'd have to get to know this woman bit by bit, piece by piece, because that was all she was going to allow until she let her guard down.

"Why is falling in love impossible?"

She sighed as they continued walking. "*Falling* in love isn't the problem," she murmured. "It's the staying in love part that I don't have much faith in."

"I have two parents, four grandparents, and about fifty aunts, uncles, cousins and friends who'd say you're wrong about that."

She finally turned to really look at him, a hard, skeptical glint appearing in those big brown eyes. That was when he knew—the woman had been burned. Badly. The realization made something twist inside him, deep down, to the nice-guy core who detested the jerks who hurt women.

"And I have a father, a sister, a couple of former stepmothers, several cousins, aunts, uncles and friends who say I'm right."

He gaped. "Not a single successful marriage in the bunch?"

Her gaze shifted, her lashes lowering over suddenly sad eyes. "My parents were supposedly happy."

Confused, he waited for her to continue.

"My mother died when I was very young. My father once said the years he spent with her were the most blissful of his life."

"So it is possible."

"They were only married for five years before she got sick."

"God, you're a pessimist."

"And you're an optimist?"

"Hell, yes. My glass may only hold beer instead of champagne, but it's almost always half full."

Jake had seen too much sadness and tragedy in his work to let himself feel anything but intensely grateful for all the good things in his life. His family, the great childhood, his job, his friends.

And now…well, now, maybe Madeline Turner. If only she'd let him get close enough to find out.

"So, what do you want to grab for lunch?" he asked, still not telling her he intended to get her to the park so she could unwind, unbend, maybe let her guard down a little.

He wanted to see the breeze off the lake blowing in her hair. Wanted to see another genuine smile, maybe even a flash of unguarded interest, as he'd seen in her eyes earlier in her office. Just like the flash that she had obviously seen the other night when they'd met.

Women hated being objectified, he knew that. And Jake had never—ever—treated any woman like a sexy body with a head stuck on it. But pausing to appreciate the soft, mouthwatering curves on this particular one had been as instinctive to him as drawing in his next breath of fresh June air.

She'd noticed. He'd noticed her noticing. Even now his hands tightened and his mouth hungered at the thought of watching her shimmy out of that glittering blue cocktail dress she'd had on.

He'd wager she'd been wearing something very black, very silky and *very* sinful underneath it. The thought of exactly what that might have looked like against the unbelievably lush curves of her body had been enough to keep his imagination racing and his libido roaring throughout the long, sleepless night after she'd left.

He sensed tonight wouldn't be much better, though she couldn't look more different than she had then. Today, dressed in her businesswoman's armor—a tailored light blue suit, silky blouse, skirt short enough to show a stunning pair of legs, but not so short that she'd send a man into cardiac arrest—she looked entirely in control. Every hint of the sexy, almost-impulsive woman who'd cut through all the bullshit games and bid a small fortune for an evening with him was gone. She had been replaced by a smooth, impeccably mannered businesswoman.

The completely unflappable professional was still incredibly hot. And the idea of *un*smoothing her, tempting her into forgetting her manners and her reserve and going wild—with *him*—already had his pants fitting a little tighter than they'd been this morning.

She was a contradiction…ice maiden and sexy, earthy woman in midnight-blue. He wanted them both. Badly.

"We really don't have to continue this facade."

"What facade?"

"This…impromptu lunch. Obviously you were startled into making the offer when my father showed up."

He grinned. "The best part was that you were startled into accepting it."

Her face flushed the tiniest bit, but she waved a hand, as if shooing a pesky little insect—or that pesky little detail—away. "Whatever the case, my father's office is on the twentieth floor. He's not watching to make sure we really are going on a date."

"Don't consider it a date," he conceded. "Let's call it a lunch meeting. Just a casual get-together so we can figure out our *real* date."

Her back stiffened. "*That's* not a real date, either."

"What would you call it?"

"A planned meeting."

"Sounds cold. What about a shared experience between two friends?"

"We're not friends."

"Maybe we will be by the time we go out." Today would, hopefully, be the start of that.

"Let's call it a…business arrangement."

"Business arrangement?" He couldn't help snorting a laugh, wondering if she had any idea what she was implying. "You know, in some circles, a woman paying a huge sum of money for a man to take her out, saying she wanted a *business arrangement*, could be construed as something very naughty."

She stopped, turning her head to look up at him. Behind them, an impatient businessman humphed but followed the pedestrian traffic as it immediately separated into two streams and went around them. Her dark eyes flashed almost black, despite the brightness of the June day. "There's nothing naughty about this, Mr. Wallace. I'm not in the market for anything like *that*."

Well, he certainly hoped not. Not only because he sure wasn't up for playing any reverse *Pretty Woman* games, but also because there was no way this woman would ever need to pay a man to spend time with her. *Any* man would want to be with Maddy, despite the tall, self-protective wall of ice she kept firmly in place around herself. And not just for her money or her background, or for the beautiful exterior package.

There was a smiling, laughing, earthy and passionate woman lurking inside her. He knew it. "Of course not."

She went on as if she hadn't heard him. "I went to that auction because I wanted to give some needy kids a good Christmas. Having to share an evening with you was entirely incidental."

Lifting one brow, he had to ask, "Why couldn't you just mail a check?"

Her mouth opened, but quickly snapped closed again. And for the first time since he'd laid eyes on her from behind that curtain, Jake realized the woman was completely flustered. Speechless. He'd *finally* gotten the best of her.

But he didn't revel in it. Instead of tormenting her with it, Jake merely took her arm, and resumed their walk, glancing occasionally at her face and seeing by the way her lips moved that she was mentally composing a cutting retort. Even though it was far too late to make one.

Jake couldn't keep a tiny smile from his mouth. Damn, he was going to enjoy watching this woman lose her self-protective shell, even if he took a few hits in the process.

Maddy Turner was most definitely worth it.

4

LYING IN A DEEP TUB of bubbles in a bathroom awash with candlelight that night, Maddy tried to empty her mind. She slowly sipped from a glass of wine and let the water ease away her cares and worries, hoping one of her greatest pleasures would distract her from the thoughts running rampant through her head. She'd been soaking for a half hour, adding hot water when it became lukewarm, nursing the glass so she wouldn't have to step out too early.

Her mind, however, wasn't cooperating. Instead it kept going over the lunch she'd shared with Jake today.

It was lunch. Just a planning meeting, as he said. Didn't mean a thing and their ball game date on Tuesday would be exactly the same way.

"Liar," she murmured, sinking deeper, watching the way the slick water caressed the curves of her breasts, making her skin shimmer and gleam in the candlelight.

It had been far more than just a business meeting. First off, most of her business meetings did not take place on a bench in the park surrounded by happy Chicagoans. Nor did they usually entail her actually *eating* anything rather than grabbing a protein bar on her way to the next appointment.

She'd never have imagined such a thing, but he hadn't given her a chance to refuse. He'd led her where he wanted her to go, as easily as he'd taken her arm to usher her across the street.

Maddy wasn't used to letting any man take the lead. But while she'd never admit it out loud, she had *almost* enjoyed it.

"Almost?" she whispered. "When did you become such a liar?"

Jake could have been a jerk after teasing her into silence about mailing a check rather than attending the auction. But he hadn't been. He'd made her relax. He'd made her smile. Made all her inhibitions disappear, at least for a little while.

How?

She had no answer. She only knew that all these hours later, even after returning to the bank for meetings and endless paperwork, she hadn't been able to forget the way his hand had felt on her arm, and the solidness of his body against hers as they'd sat on that park bench.

That's not the only place you wanted his hand.

No, it wasn't. Blowing at a bubble on the puckered tip of her breast, she reached up and lightly brushed it away, acknowledging, at least here in the privacy of her bathroom, how much she wanted the hand on her body to be Jake's. Her fingers were slender and soft, smooth and easy as they slid down, beneath the water, gliding across her wet skin. His were big and strong and would feel deliciously rough.

"Especially *here*," she whispered, closing her eyes as she touched herself even more intimately.

In her mind, though, the touch was all his. And within moments, the possibilities playing in her mind had her thrusting against her own fingers, longing to be filled but taking the only form of pleasure she could manage at the moment. Maddy sighed, gasped, stroked the lips of her sex and the hard nub of flesh at the top of it, wondering how on earth she'd gone for so long without a man's hands on her.

"Not just any man's," she reminded herself. There was only one pair of hands she wanted. One mouth. One body. One person she visualized as she spiraled toward a climax.

The tension built like a carefully tended fire before erupting in a soft wave of pleasure that had her shaking and gasping for breath, even as she whispered one word, over and over.

His name.

She hadn't even floated back to earth when she was interrupted by a stark ringing sound. Jerking like a kid caught playing with herself under the covers, Maddy sat bolt upright, her hand flying instinctively to the receiver.

She'd thought it incredibly silly to have a phone in the bathroom when she'd bought this condo last year. Looking back, however, she knew it was a good thing. She did enjoy her baths.

"Hello?"

"How did it go? Have you done him yet?"

Tabby. She should have known. She'd lay money her father had pronounced it to the world when she'd left for a lunch date today. Sinking back down in the water, she replied, "It was lunch. *Just* lunch."

"But with *him*, right?"

Tabby had already pumped her for all the details of the bachelor auction, calling her late the night it had taken place. Maddy had somehow managed to remain noncommittal, pretending it had gone as planned and she hadn't been affected by her *prize*.

"Maddy? Come on, spill. You did have lunch with that darkhaired, dark-eyed stud from the auction, didn't you?"

"How do you know what he looks like?"

Her sister made a dismissive sound. "You probably described him really well on the phone."

Possible, though Maddy remembered trying to be extremely nondescriptive and brief, not wanting to ever think about Jake Wallace again after that night. But she supposed she could have waxed a little poetic about the guy, under Tabby's relentless prodding.

But something in her sister's tone—a note of mischief, of

amusement—made her suspect it wasn't true. "I don't think I described him that well."

Silence.

And suddenly she figured it out. Gasping, she sat straight up in the tub again, nearly dropping the phone into the mountain of bubbles. "You were there!"

"Don't be ridiculous…"

"You came to the auction. Despite all your claims about how you couldn't be trusted and I had to be the one to do it, you went anyway."

"Well, I couldn't very well send you up against a professional without making sure you were okay."

Against a professional… Mmm, she could think of worse places to be than up against that man's rock-hard body. Especially after having experienced what just *fantasizing* about him could make her feel.

"After all, you are my baby sister."

That was about one layer too thick. "Bullshit. I bet you were the one who told him how to find me, even after I intentionally left without giving him my name."

"I don't know what you're talking about."

Yeah, right.

"And don't try to claim you were looking out for me," Maddy added. "You were dying of curiosity."

As usual, when busted, Tabitha didn't even try to act repentant. "Well, it's not every day all the rich bitches of this town go into heat over the same hound dog."

"He's not a…" She quickly bit her tongue, not wanting to give Tabby any more ammunition.

Too late. "Whoa-ho! You're falling for him!"

"Of course I'm not."

"But you want him."

"Of course I do." Maddy wasn't one to prevaricate, either.

"So what's the problem? Take him. You are in such desperate need of a good fuck you might as well be wearing a Please Take Me sign."

"Charming. Do you kiss your fiancé with that mouth?"

"My future husband is very proper. He hasn't yet learned of the miraculous things I can do with my mouth," Tabby said with a catlike purr. "But seriously, you know you want to have sex with that guy."

"Any woman would," she admitted.

"Of course they would. He's gorgeous. It really is a good thing I talked you into doing it. I wouldn't have been able to walk out of the hotel without at least a little taste."

A little taste. Sounded yummy. Only, she knew it wouldn't be nearly enough. That would be like offering a four-year-old a little taste of his own birthday cake.

"And I really can't afford one more broken engagement. I'll get a reputation."

"You love your reputation. And so do all the men who want to be the one to make you settle down."

Tabby chuckled. "Maybe." Then she lowered her voice, sounding serious—tender—for a change. "But I really don't want to do anything to risk losing Brad. He…he calms me. Settles me. And I think he's exactly what I need."

That explained a lot. Honestly, Maddy had wondered about Tabby's latest choice in husband. Because, though he was extremely wealthy, Tabby's soon-to-be-hubby was average looking and staid compared to the other men she'd been involved with.

"You might be right," Maddy murmured, smiling at the thought of her wild-child sibling truly settling down.

The serious, tender sister quickly disappeared. "Maybe you can bring the stud-muffin to the wedding. Wouldn't Deborah just choke on her chateaubriand?"

Shaking her head, Maddy said, "I'm hanging up now."

"No, I want details."

"I'm in the tub."

"Alone?"

"Of course alone." She might have said that a bit too sharply.

"Bet you wish you weren't. Are you…keeping yourself company?"

Was it possible for someone to hear a person blush? "Don't be ridiculous."

Tabby's throaty laugh said how much she believed that one. "Oooh, little sister's having a date with her shower massage."

God. "I'm hanging up…"

"Didn't mean to interrupt. Don't do anything I wouldn't do."

"That would be utterly impossible."

"True. Remember to call me after your *real* date. You are going, aren't you?"

Hating to admit it, she said, "Tuesday afternoon."

"And hopefully it will last into Wednesday morning. Call me just as soon as he leaves. I want to know—"

But before Tabby could finish, Maddy hung up the phone. Shaking her head, she sank back down into the cooling tub of water, now wanting the rapidly disappearing bubbles to wash away her humiliation.

Her first time in ages doing something to take the edge off and she got busted. Absolutely the only thing that could have been worse would have been if Jake had been the one who'd called.

Then she thought about it. Jake calling while she'd been touching herself. Whispers on the phone. Shared fantasies. Secret desires.

And she reached for the handle, sending another stream of hot, steamy water into the tub.

THE INTRINSIC INNER "gentleman" who had been pounded into Jake's personality since he was a kid rebelled at meeting Maddy for their date, rather than going to her place and knocking on her door. There had been a rule growing up in his house—dates, especially first dates, came inside and got the full family third degree, or nobody went anywhere. More than one of his sisters' boyfriends had been introduced to their father while he was wearing his camouflage hunting gear and cleaning his shotgun.

But *not* coming to the door was worse, as one of his younger sister Jenny's boyfriends could attest. The first time he'd tried beeping from his car, their father had gone outside, reached in through the passenger side window and attached The Club to the pimple-faced teenager's steering wheel.

He wondered what his old man would make of Maddy Turner. He didn't wonder for long. Hell, nobody in his family was judgmental. They'd see past the name and the family connection to the woman beneath.

Just as Jake had.

They judged a person by his or her character, not their bank balance. And a good character meant being courteous…bringing flowers for a date, knocking, holding doors.

None of which he was allowed to do today.

But when he saw Maddy leaning against a sporty little car in the commuter parking lot where they'd arranged to meet, he forgot about that concern. A smile slowly widened his lips as he studied her, head to toe, acknowledging that the woman looked even better in cute-knee length pants, a hot pink tank top and a ball cap with her ponytail hanging out the hole in the back than she had in her silky blue cocktail dress.

"See?" she said as he parked beside her and got out of his pickup. "I do own something other than a suit or an evening dress."

Right. He'd wager the sleeveless top came from one of those high-end shops on the Magnificent Mile and had probably cost as much as Jake spent on clothes in a month. It was too deceptively simple to actually be cheap.

Simple…but way sexy.

"You look very cute."

Wrong thing to say. Her lips twisted the tiniest bit.

"I mean, very pretty."

"I was going for girl-next-door."

"Sure. You look just like the girl who lives next door to Bill Gates."

"Are you going to harass me about being rich all day?"

"Well, it's better than being harassed for being poor, isn't it?"

"As if you'd know anything about that?"

They hadn't really talked much about his family, beyond him admitting it was big, so he didn't take offense. "Believe me, I grew up strictly blue collar, middle class. My family never lived in the lap of luxury. More like the lap of just-enough-to-get-by."

She stared at him, her lips slightly pursed, as if assessing the truth of his words. "Which probably gave you the drive to succeed, to be financially stable on your own, no matter what you had to do to make it happen."

He chuckled. If he'd wanted money, he would have gone on to medical school, as he'd considered doing after college. Paramedics weren't exactly rolling in the green stuff. "My job's not what you'd consider—"

She put her hand up, palm out. "I don't want to hear the gory details about your *job*. We're keeping this entirely impersonal, aren't we?"

Touchy, touchy. But he let her get away with it. Aside from the fact that some people truly were squeamish about medical stuff—which *could* be gory—Maddy had put that wall back up in place around herself. He had to slowly ease his way over it as he had the other day when they'd gone for their picnic lunch. With small, easy steps.

Seeing a tiny price tag still hanging from the side of her

brightly colored ball cap, he reached up and tugged it free. "Went shopping, huh?"

She snagged the corner of that full bottom lip between her teeth. "It's my first professional game," she whispered. "I wanted to look the part."

"Your first ball game? Are you kidding?" Suddenly realizing something, he murmured, "I'm sorry, if you're really not interested, we could do something else."

"No way! I love baseball. But I never got the chance to go see a game in person."

"I'm surprised your bank doesn't have a box."

"We do. But that's so…removed from everything. I can just as easily sit in my living room and watch it on TV. If I'm going in person, I want to sit in the stands, and eat peanuts and drink beer, glare at drunks spitting in the next row and yell at the ump when he makes a bad call."

Yep. Pretty typical ball game, in Jake's experience. "Well, then, I think you bid on the right man."

She shifted her eyes away, mumbling something.

"What?"

"Nothing." Then she glanced at his pickup. "Do you want to take my car? You can drive."

"Sorry. I don't drive chick cars." He headed for the passenger seat instead. "But I guess it won't kill my reputation to be seen riding in one."

She rolled her eyes. "I'll warn you to keep your head down when we're coming up to any crowded intersection. We wouldn't want to damage your…reputation."

She got in beside him, and in the close confines of the tiny car, he suddenly noticed the sweet, light fragrance of her skin. The fruity scent of her hair. And the earthier scent of pure, unadulterated woman.

He was, quite simply, unable to resist her any longer.

"Maddy?"

She had reached for the ignition, but paused, turning to give him her full attention. "Yes?"

"I know this isn't exactly protocol for a first date. But I can't help it."

"Help what?"

"Help this," he whispered. And without another word, he leaned over, caressed her smooth cheek with the tips of his fingers, and covered her beautiful, soft lips with his own.

She tensed for the slightest moment, then, with a little sigh of acceptance, relaxed. The tension left her jaw, the stiffness departed from her mouth, and she parted her lips slightly, to share a warm breath with him.

Jake inhaled it, tasting her, letting himself be filled by her essence. The kiss remained light, sweet, innocent. They were joined only by the softest brush of lips and scrape of his fingers on her cheek. And he knew that despite how desperately he wanted to sink his tongue into her for a fuller taste, he couldn't deny himself the sweetness of this simple, innocent pleasure.

Finally, when he no longer trusted himself to keep it simple and innocent, he slowly pulled away. "I'm sorry."

"Sorry you kissed me?" she whispered, blinking a few times as if she'd just awakened from a dream.

He shook his head. "Sorry I had to stop."

"Oh."

He shifted in his seat, trying to stretch his long legs in the cramped front seat, wondering if she'd noticed how much *tighter* the fit was now that he'd let himself give in to the need to taste her. Especially the fit of his jeans.

"That was *supposed* to be a friendly kiss hello."

"Aren't those usually on the cheek?"

"I think they're usually in the air an inch from the cheek in your social set, aren't they?"

She nodded, her choppy, audible breaths finally slowing as she, too, returned to normal. "Yes." Then, not meeting his eye, she added, "But I think I like your way better."

THE AFTERNOON was everything Maddy had dreamed it would be. Her twenty-five thousand dollars had bought her nosebleed seats at a game the Cubs were about to lose. But it didn't matter. She was so excited to be in the crowd, experiencing live Major League Baseball the way she'd always imagined it would be, that she simply didn't care.

Jake treated her like the girl-next-door she'd proclaimed herself to be. And he—despite his supposedly international up-bringing, which she'd seen absolutely *no* evidence of since they'd met—was playing the role of all-American boy as if he'd invented it. It was hard to believe he was anything other than a normal, hardworking guy from any small town, rather than a paid escort competed over by rich women.

Maybe Tabby made a mistake.

No. It wasn't a mistake. She'd told Maddy the exact number, and their stepmother and her cronies had bid like wild women on Bachelor Number Nineteen. Plus, from what Maddy remembered about his bio in the program, it had said he liked to travel the world in search of beautiful women and sexy adventures.

Not quite like the guy cheering on the home team beside her. So he obviously wore a different persona depending on the situation. She honestly didn't know, however, which was the real man.

"Want some peanuts?" he asked, already flagging down a vendor.

"I think that was on my list of requirements for today," she admitted.

Jake grinned, put an icy-cold beer in her hand, and glared down anyone around them who got too close with their wildly gesticulating arms and elbows.

He also kept up a running commentary on the game, explaining all the plays. She let him. It seemed such an innate man thing—the need to explain sports to the little woman—that she didn't have the heart to tell him she'd been a star of her college fast-pitch softball team. She'd even thought about going further with it and shooting for the national team.

Maddy might be soft from several years working in the bank, but she'd once been pretty damned athletic. She'd even considered breast reduction surgery. Sport bras did not do much to help a woman with a D cup. Her teammates used to joke that one day, if she bounced too much as she ran, she'd knock herself out.

Maddy had given up her Olympic hopes when her father had gone through his last divorce, from his third wife. Maddy had been so worried about him, she'd decided to go home after graduation, rather than pursue that dream.

Which meant her breasts were safe. And prominent enough to draw the gawking attention of a few guys around her. She'd heard the comments from a creep sitting behind her for the last half hour, but was quite adept at ignoring them. She'd had lots of practice.

Jake, however, had not.

After the slurred voice behind her got loud enough for Jake to hear it over the crowd, he leaped to his feet, turned around and thrust an angry finger into the drunk man's face. "Didn't your mother ever teach you to keep your eyes to your own damn self and your fat mouth closed?" he snapped.

The foulmouthed fan, a heavyset, sweaty guy with red cheeks and beer-scented breath, rose, too, swaying on his feet. "Hey man, she's hot."

"She's also not deaf," Maddy murmured, turning in her seat to watch. She'd be damned if she would rise to her feet to prevent the jackass from leering down her shirt some more. It wasn't low-cut. And she didn't have a single thing to be ashamed of.

"You're hot," the guy repeated as he gaped from above.

"So you said."

Despite the crudeness she'd heard from the stranger before Jake had caught on and launched at him, she remained more annoyed than offended. Leave it to a breast-obsessed little boy wearing men's triple-X sized clothing to ruin her lovely afternoon.

It wasn't as though she'd never experienced it before. A woman with her build had to either get used to men treating her like a walking pair of breasts or spend her entire life in a constant state of annoyance.

He gave Maddy a bleary smile, still oblivious to the depth of Jake's anger. "Bet if you flash 'em, the camera'll focus in on ya and put ya up on the big screen."

"Oh, and I live for just such a moment."

"You must not like your teeth very much, buddy," Jake snapped. "Keep talking and you're going to be saying goodbye to quite a few of them."

Maddy had become adept at retaliating against offensive men, even if, quite often, her put-downs went right over their imbecilic heads. "Please, Jake, let it go," she added. "I'm quite sure that in the world of this gentleman's favorite show, *The Girls Next Door*, he's behaving with absolutely perfect gentility."

"Hey! That *is* my favorite show!"

Uh-huh. Right over his poor wee imbecilic head.

She almost laughed—until she realized Jake was not merely angry, he was downright furious. Rage flashed behind his eyes and his tightly clenched body seemed ready to lash out. He appeared capable of real violence, all because some stupid drunk had opened his mouth.

The stupid drunk was apparently too far gone to realize he was about two inches from death-by-enraged-gigolo. "They're real, ain't they?"

"Sit down," Maddy snapped, finally starting to lose her

patience. She grabbed Jake's arm, stopping him midgrowl as he began to climb over the back of his seat. "You, too. Before you get us all thrown out."

"Maddy…"

She kept her hand on his arm, her nails digging in tight, determined to handle this situation herself. Without violence. Though, she had to admit, a teeny, tiny part of her liked how protective Jake was, even if she usually had absolutely no use for such blatant displays of testosterone.

"You. Sit. I mean it," she ordered the intoxicated stranger, pointing to his seat.

The man sat.

"Now, I'm quite certain that somewhere in your beer-sodden brain, you believe I'm flattered by your eloquently worded… *compliments*." Maddy didn't have to raise her voice to make sure she was being heard. All around them, conversations had quieted, and she didn't think a single spectator in their section was watching what was going on down in the field. The showdown here was apparently much more interesting.

"However, while I'm sure you are a man who possesses many admirable porcine qualities, as you can see, I *am* here in the company of another gentleman. And neither of us appreciates your attentions. Will you please, therefore, refrain from commenting further and allow us to get back to the game?"

The man's mouth fell open. "What'd she say?"

The embarrassed-looking man next to him—his friend who'd made no effort to provide backup to the drunk—muttered, "I'm pretty sure she told you to shut the hell up."

"Yeah," someone else said. "So please do us all a favor and do it!"

"Oh," the drunk said, finally glancing around and realizing what a spectacle he'd made of himself. If Maddy had railed at him, he probably wouldn't have backed down. As it was, though, her calm, courteous reply made him look an absolute fool. And he wasn't too drunk to realize it.

"Sorry," he mumbled.

"Thank you." Maddy smiled and nodded politely, then turned back around to face the field, putting a definite end to the interaction. It was the top of the ninth and things were getting interesting. She wasn't going to waste another moment of the beautiful day on a blithering fool.

She didn't even glance over as Jake slowly dropped back into his seat beside her. "I can take care of myself, you know," she murmured, watching the field.

"Yeah, I noticed." Jake leaned closer, near enough for her to feel the warmth of his breath on her hair. Not to mention the way his shoulders shook with laughter. His anger had disappeared as quickly as steam off a bathroom mirror. "Correct me if I'm wrong…did you just call him a pig?"

"I'm certain I don't know what you mean."

"Uh-huh. Sure you don't."

Still chuckling, Jake casually dropped his big, solid hand onto her thigh, above her knee, and squeezed it. Not exactly the most erogenous zone on her body, but still, every molecule inside her leaped to attention. Her blood roared in her veins at the feel of that strong, warm touch, and she was completely incapable of stopping the visual images that flooded her mind.

Maddy's skin tingled beneath the soft fabric of her capris at the thought of him sliding that touch higher, caressing her all the way up her thigh as he kissed her again, just as he had in the car. Slow, sweet…then deeper, harder. Wetter and faster.

She wanted him to kiss her in every way a man could kiss a woman. And in every place on her body.

God, she was a wreck. Yet he seemed completely unaffected, still smiling that easygoing smile. "Remind me never to get on your bad side. I'm slightly more literate than our friend back there. And I do believe that tongue of yours could draw blood if the person actually understood what the hell you were saying."

Maddy tried to force her heart to slow its rapid pace, striving for the same nonchalance Jake obviously felt about his casually possessive touch on her leg.

She didn't succeed. Her pulse still raced, her breaths grew fast and uneven. She couldn't tear her gaze away from the strong, deeply tanned fingers starkly outlined against her clothing.

Then, thank heaven, she was saved. Because with the bases loaded, the next player at bat hit one out of the park. The entire stadium roared, rising to its feet as if one huge, sinuous being, Maddy and Jake among them.

Whoever that player was, she could kiss him, she really could. Because somehow, during the euphoric celebrations of the home team's victory, she managed to calm down and put all her protective gear firmly back in place.

Almost through, she reminded herself. Their date was almost done, then she could forget about this day, forget about him. Seeing the way he'd been completely unaffected by a simple touch that had left her breathless had reminded her of just who she was dealing with her. This man dealt in intimate touches and was completely unaffected by them.

She, however, was not, and would never be. Which meant she needed to put an end to this ridiculous date. And get back to her regularly scheduled life.

5

SITTING AT A GOUGED and pitted oak table at a popular downtown pub that evening, Jake watched carefully for the first sign that Maddy wasn't enjoying herself. So far, he'd seen absolutely nothing. Not even her run-in with the obnoxious drunk at the stadium had affected her.

He still wanted to laugh when he thought about it. He'd seen women erupt on rude men, had witnessed his baby sister throw a glass vase at her boyfriend's head. But he'd never seen one completely emasculate a guy with her mouth…without the idiot ever even realizing it.

Most impressive.

"I can't believe I'm eating like this."

They'd been munching on chicken wings and a mountain of nachos. And to his surprise, Maddy had opted for beer, sharing a half pitcher with him, instead of some sweet, girlie drink. She seemed relaxed. If not outright laughing, she at least smiled more than once.

"Don't be too hard on yourself. I don't think they even serve salads here, unless they're topped with deep-fried chicken and a mountain of cheese."

One fine, delicate brow arched and she stared at him with quiet reproach, though a hint of a smile lurked on her beautiful mouth. "What are you suggesting, Jake? That I should only be eating salads?"

He backpedaled, holding up a quick, defensive hand. Damn, how could guys avoid these basic traps women always set out for them? "No way." Grinning, he added, "Just seems like the only things my sisters ever ordered. God forbid one of them should ever have taken a bite out of a hamburger, especially if one of their boyfriends was around."

"It's a female thing." She sighed heavily, as if accepting something that was inevitable. "Not just the instinct to watch what we eat, so we can look like what all the media images *tell* us we should look like. There's also a need to eat lightly in front of men, as if we need to assure them we're on top of things and will never gain weight."

"When secretly you're all dying for wings and nachos?"

She licked her lips, then smacked them together before reaching for another. "Yes. Any of your sisters married?"

"The oldest, with three kids—twin boys and a girl. And Blair, who's a year older than me, is engaged."

"Uh-huh. Watch her at the wedding reception. She's going to bite into the first piece of cake she's had since she decided he was *the one*, and will look like she's already had her first orgasm of the night."

Knowing his big sister, Maddy was probably right. Then the orgasm part of her statement kicked in and he coughed into his fist.

She didn't even seem to notice. "Which is why most new wives gain a few pounds in the first year of marriage, not including the weight of the rock on their hand."

"So should I be flattered that you're on your fourth wing? You don't need to worry about impressing me?" He wondered what she'd say if she knew he was more impressed by her adorable honesty and the way she licked the tips of her fingers after each nibble. *Yum*.

"Exactly. Because this is not a legitimate date."

"Says you."

"Says me."

"What if it was?"

She snorted an inelegant laugh that sounded completely unlike her, but incredibly cute. "Then I would have asked for a bread stick and a glass of water."

He *knew* this one. "With lemon!"

"Of course. Natural diuretic." She wagged her eyebrows, a very un-Maddylike move. "You're good."

"Hello, three sisters?"

"*Three?* Goodness, you do get a lot of torment."

She had no idea. The older two used to dress him up as a baby doll and play with him when they were kids. Usually choosing to dress him as a girl. Not that he was about to tell *her* that.

"What if I wanted it to be?" he asked.

"Wanted it to be what?"

Knowing he was pushing it, but realizing he had an opening provided by the beer or two, which had helped her loosen up, he plunged forward. "A real date."

She shook her head, dipping the appetizer into a tiny dish of blue cheese dressing. "Not an option."

Wow, talk about shooting a guy down without a moment's hesitation. But Jake didn't worry…the night was young. He had a few hours to change her mind.

Besides, he knew where she worked. She'd soon find out that he didn't give up on something he wanted quite that easily. And he most definitely wanted her. More with every minute that passed.

He risked a quick, appreciative look across the table at her curvy figure, so incredibly sexy in her hot pink top. "By the way, in my opinion you don't have a *thing* to worry about."

"Ha. I have huge breasts, short legs, what my father likes to call my late mother's 'childbearing hips' and a big backside."

As if any man would complain about a single one of those

things? Was she for real? "Honey from where I'm sitting, you are just about perfect."

"From where you're sitting, you can't *see* the extra fifteen pounds that couldn't be removed from my body by a plastic surgeon using an industrial Shop-Vac instead of a liposuction machine."

He barked a quick laugh. "You're not going to get an agreement from any man alive on that score, Madeline Turner. You are shaped exactly the way a woman should be shaped."

"Uh-huh," she said, disbelief ringing clearly in her voice. "Tell that to the Chicago Club set who have replica Paris fashion models on their arms."

"You're beautiful," he said firmly, not allowing her to argue it. Thinking about what she'd said, he added, "And if you let some quack touch you I'll have to hunt him down and put a hurt on him."

"Are you always so aggressive?"

"Are you always so hard on yourself?"

That appeared to shock her. Maddy's mouth dropped open, as if he'd accused her of having an extra limb. "Hard on myself? *Me?* I've got a well-known reputation as a self-confident ice queen."

"Maybe in the financial world." He reached across the table and smoothed back a long, silky strand of hair that had escaped her ponytail, touching her cheek lightly in the process. "Not in the real one."

Maddy froze for a moment, allowing the brief caress. Then, as he could have predicted, she carefully slid away from it, as if realizing she'd been getting far too comfortable around him. Now she was putting that distance back—that wall.

He didn't take it personally. Especially because he had realized something—the separation wasn't just between her and him, but between her and *everyone.* As if she constantly had to keep a shield in place to prevent anyone from getting too close. Or from getting too obnoxious, like the guy at the ballpark, whom she had so easily put in his place.

He knew from experience that the absolute worst thing to do with a woman who already had her guard up was to try to stampede through it. Which was why he'd downplayed that casual touch at the stadium. Jeez, he'd meant to offer her a way-to-go squeeze but had ended up completely dumbstruck by the way the simple brush of his hand against her leg had made him feel.

Awed. Hot. Out of his mind hungry.

And he'd had to pretend he'd felt absolutely *nothing*. Or risk adding to the armor he'd finally begun to slowly chip away.

"I have plenty of self-confidence. Just because I don't appear on the social pages with a different man every week doesn't mean I don't know I'm moderately attractive."

Attractive didn't even begin to describe her.

"I don't have the time or the energy for any of that romantic nonsense."

"So who was he?" he asked, not even looking into her eyes as he reached for his beer.

"Who was who?"

"The guy who gave you such a negative outlook on love."

He wondered for a moment if she would take offense, but her soft laughter told him she hadn't. "Uh, remember who you're talking to? Jason Turner's daughter sitting over here?"

Jake had brought his mug to his mouth but hadn't yet sipped. He slowly lowered it. "Your father is the one who convinced you you're better off being alone?"

"For the most part." Her eyes shifted, she wasn't telling the whole story, but at least she was opening up a little.

He wasn't willing to risk her shutting down by pushing into areas she didn't want to discuss. Still, she'd brought it up— again. She'd mentioned her father's romantic issues during their walk. "Just because he's had some bad luck?"

"I've seen my father fall in and out of love so many times the word has simply lost its meaning. I've come to realize he's in love with being in love." Her mouth twisted. "Then there's Tabby, my sister."

The name hinted at what she was probably like. "Older or younger?"

"Older. Divorced once, on her second engagement since. She hasn't quite nailed down that true love thing, either, though not for lack of trying. A lot."

"And what about Madeline?"

"Not interested."

"Not even a chance you're wrong about that, huh?"

She shook her head. "Nope. Not worth it."

He pointed to her glass. "It's more than half-full."

She pointed to his. "Yours is almost empty."

"Easily remedied." Reaching for the half pitcher, he topped up his mug. "See? It's all in your perspective."

Maddy frowned, though he'd swear he saw a hint of unguarded humor in her eyes. It was quickly gone and her manner returned to aloof, unaffected, unmoved. "Perspective doesn't change fact. And I really don't know why we're even talking about this. We're here, together, because of a charity obligation, not out of any real interest or—" her voice faltered for the first time "—attraction."

"Speak for yourself."

Her pulse fluttered visibly in her throat.

"I am *incredibly* attracted to you." He knew he risked scaring her off again, but could be nothing but honest. There was no way he could allow her to go on believing he was only here because she'd bid on him at some charity event. "In case that kiss earlier didn't clue you in, let me give it to you straight. I have wanted you since I spotted you from behind the curtains the other night at the auction."

For the second time since he'd known her, Jake had managed to shock Maddy speechless. She stared at him, blinking a few times, her mouth open but no sounds coming out.

Why the hell she should be surprised, he had no idea. She had to have seen the lust in his eyes the night they met, before he'd realized she wouldn't appreciate any kind of obvious come-ons and gotten himself under control. And the woman was sexy enough to make a ninety-year-old beg his doctor for a year's supply of Viagra.

Yet she seemed entirely oblivious to it.

Color washed through her beautiful cheeks. Maddy's lips parted as she breathed across them. Even from across the table, he could see the way her chest moved with each deep inhalation.

His body reacted. The lazy hunger that had been flowing through his veins focused in tighter, right in his crotch. "You can't tell me you didn't realize it."

She swallowed, shaking her head. "I did. But I just assumed you were being…that you were used to making women feel like you wanted them, because, you know, I'd bid so much." Regaining some confidence, she leaned over and accused him with one hard stare. "You haven't looked at me *that* way all day today."

"Did you not notice that I almost tore a guy's head off because *he* looked at you *that* way."

"That's different. He was drunk and stupid and…"

"Porcine?"

"Exactly."

"I'm not a pig. I'm a gentleman." Tension snapping between them, he leaned closer, keeping his voice low and intimate. Raking a hot glance over her, he admitted, "And a gentleman doesn't come right out on a first date and tell a woman he wants to smother her beautiful nipples in sugar and then suck every bit of sweetness right out of her until she's begging to be taken."

She gasped, but he was too far gone. Both his mouth…and his body, which was now rock-hard beneath the table.

"And it wouldn't have been terribly polite of me to tell you I've been wondering all day what color panties you have on.

Whether it's a thong, whether the curves of your ass are really as round and sweet as I think they are."

"Jake…"

"Or that if I fell into your incredible breasts and smothered to death, I'd die with a smile on my face."

"Oh my."

"Or that when I touched your leg this afternoon, all I could think of was how slim your thighs are. How easily my hands would wrap around them. How amazing it would be to lift them over my shoulders, getting the best possible angle so I could plunge into you, *hard,* and fill you so completely you feel like you're gonna break in half."

"Holy shit," someone said.

It wasn't her.

Sanity returned as he realized their waitress stood beside the table, wide-eyed, pink-cheeked. And all ears. "Wow, hot stuff, if she says no, you can have my number!"

The young woman appeared entirely serious. Which didn't help things, judging by the way the woman sitting across from him narrowed her eyes and clenched her arms tightly around her chest. Small wonder…he'd verbally molested her in front of witnesses. Some fricking gentleman.

"Jesus, Maddy…"

"We're finished," she snapped, almost launching herself to her feet. She threw a fistful of cash down on the table, ignoring the waitress, who still watched them, and not sparing Jake another glance.

She didn't even wait for him, or look to see if he was following. Instead, without another word, she wove her way through the crowd toward the door, not looking left or right, her dark ponytail bouncing against her stiff shoulders with every step.

Oh, God, had he ever screwed this up.

"I'm sorry," he mumbled to the waitress.

"Don't apologize. I think I just came a little."

Jake closed his eyes and shook his head, about as embarrassed as he'd ever been in his life. Heaven help him if his sisters—or worse, his father—ever heard about this. Talk about not treating a lady right. He'd blown it, starting with the sex talk that had been overheard, and ending with her throwing down a small fortune to pay for dinner, when he would *never* have let her pick up the tab.

Wanting to crawl out of the place, he settled for a fast walk. He hit the front door with both palms and strode outside, half expecting to see Maddy's taillights as she zipped her tiny sports car out of the parking lot, dumping his butt right here at the bar.

But her car remained on the far side of the lot, where she'd parked it. He hadn't gotten more than a half-dozen steps toward it in the warm evening air when he was grabbed. Two hands bunched in the front of his T-shirt and pushed him. Jake stumbled over his own feet until he was backed against the dark, shadowy side of the old brick building.

"Maddy…"

"Shut up." Her eyes sparked and her breathing was choppy as she glared up at him. She looked ready to hit him.

Instead, she did something far more unexpected. She threw her arms around his neck, pressed that hot body against his, and caught his mouth in a deep, hard kiss.

She wasn't angry. The ice princess was on fire.

For *him*.

She kissed the taste out of his mouth, thrusting her tongue against his wildly as she tangled her fingers in the hair at the nape of his neck. Jake instinctively dropped his hands, reaching for the round curves of the ass he'd been admiring since they met. Cupping those curves, he savored the softness, squeezing her lightly. He was going to love holding her cheeks tightly when she was naked and on top of him. Plunging down onto him, over and over until he lost his mind and exploded inside her.

Tugging her up for a nicer fit, he rocked into her, letting her feel his throbbing erection, getting off at the pleasure of sex against sex, despite their clothes.

She whimpered, ground back, tilted her hips against him to bring her heat directly against the seam straining to hold back his cock. Groaning, running her hands frantically over his shoulders and chest now, she continued to play wildly in his mouth. Her soft lips molded to every millimeter of his, her tongue ravaged his as if she was hungry enough to devour him whole.

Finally, she drew away, gasping for breath, but not stopping. Oh, no, she merely moved her mouth to his neck, tasting the sweat he knew had gathered there, kissing her way frantically to the hollow of his throat, even biting lightly.

"I want you so much."

"I noticed."

"Did you really mean those things you said inside?"

He spun her around, backing her against the building now, taking control. "Hell, *yes*."

It was crazy—they were outside, in a public place, it wasn't even ten o'clock and anyone could walk out of the bar at any minute. But he didn't care. If he didn't get more of her, he'd die. Simply blow up and die.

"This really is…personal? Just about attraction, nothing else?" she asked, watching him intently, as if still needing to be sure.

"Maddy, I don't give a damn where we met, who you are, or that you bid on me for some charity. I have wanted you since the moment I set eyes on you."

She nodded slowly, letting her eyes drift closed, silently giving her assent.

"Don't stop me," he whispered hoarsely as he tugged her

ponytail holder off and ran his fingers through that thick, dark hair, spreading it across her shoulders. He tasted her soft earlobe, moving slowly down the long line of her delicate neck, nibbling lightly, savoring the unique flavors of skin and woman.

"Stopping you isn't even a consideration."

Soon he was breathing down the front of her shirt, his lips scraping the vulnerable skin just above the seam. Unable to resist, he nudged the fabric down enough to gain access, groaning when he saw a hint of her breasts rising above the edge of a hot pink bra.

He *had* to go further. Running the tip of his tongue across that deep line of cleavage, he grabbed her hips when she started to sag.

"Jake…"

"More." He didn't ask, didn't think, didn't hesitate. He merely reached for the bottom of her shirt and began to tug it up. He was dying to touch her, hold her, suck her.

She whimpered when he slid his hand inside the bra, cupping her, tugging the incredibly soft, warm mound free of its containment. Then he could only look at her, wondering if he'd ever seen a more beautiful woman—with her head thrown back, eyes wild, hair a tangled brown mass. Her lips were wet, her mouth open, and her full, gorgeous breast was topped by a puckered pink nipple that begged to be tasted.

"No sugar handy," he mumbled, "but I know you're sweet enough."

Then he confirmed it, covering the taut tip with his mouth and sucking, quick, hard, not sure which of them was more shocked by the pleasure of it.

God knows how far he might have taken it…they were both that far gone. But a car suddenly turned into the parking lot, washing the outside entrance with light. It spilled to within a foot of where they stood as the vehicle turned into a corner parking spot.

"Help me," she snapped, desperately trying to yank her bra back in place.

He did, pushing her hands out of the way and, with regret, covering those incredible curves. Edging around, he blocked the view of her body with his own. If anybody did spy them, all they'd see was a couple kissing in the shadows.

A trio of laughing young women passed within a few feet of them, exchanging loud, knowing whispers. Once they were gone, he stared down at a still wide-eyed Maddy and offered her a slow, knowing smile. "You ready to get out of here?"

She nibbled on her bottom lip for a split second, nearly giving him a heart attack as he feared she was getting cold feet.

He should have known better. Because, with pure, sexual determination on her face, she grabbed his hand and dragged him to her car. "You drive," she snapped. "I know you don't like chick cars, but my legs are shaking too much."

She tossed him the keys, which he caught in midair. Opening the passenger side door for her, he helped her in, bending low to ask, "Where are we going?"

She muttered an uptown address.

"I don't think that's where we left my truck." He didn't know why he got such a kick out of teasing her, especially because, honestly, if she walked away from him now, he'd have to go douse himself in liquid hydrogen to cool off.

"It's my place. It's close. I have an *enormous* bed and an incredible bathroom."

He smiled slowly. "I'm catching the vision."

"My bathtub could fit three people."

"Sorry, Ms. Turner, not into anything kinky." When her eyes widened, he took pity and grinned. "I'm sure we can make full use of it, just the two of us."

"Good." She ran the tip of one finger across his bottom lip. "Now get in and *drive*."

SHE SHOULD BE having regrets, or at least second thoughts. But as they drove into the night—Jake's foot riding a little heavier on the gas pedal than hers usually did—she could only anticipate.

He wanted her. Just *wanted* her. Those dark eyes hadn't been appraising her worth; he hadn't been using any tried-and-true lines of seduction that had worked on the many women in his past. Hadn't for one second made her feel that she was nothing but a client to him. But he *had* made her feel absolutely dizzy with desire.

Her reservations had begun to dissipate when he'd thrown that line about dipping her nipples in sugar. By the time he'd gotten to the breaking her in half part, she'd been practically stuck to her chair.

Unable to wait, she reached over and dropped her hand onto his leg.

"Uh-uh," he growled.

She ignored him, sliding her hand higher. But before she could capture the bulging prize she desperately wanted to trace with her fingertips, he dropped his hand over hers and squeezed.

"No."

"You don't want me to touch you?" she whispered, knowing the words were untrue. Despite the shadowy interior of the car, she could *see* just how much he wanted her touch. And, judging by the way he'd felt when pressed against her, he had a lot to be touched.

She shivered in her seat.

"Hell, yes, I want you to touch me."

She twisted more, her other hand reaching for his hip. He couldn't stop her…couldn't drive no-handed.

"But *not* at the risk of both of us getting killed." He glanced over, serious, almost pleading with her to back off. "Please, babe, we'll be there soon, I promise. I've seen way too many street wrecks to even consider doing something so unsafe, despite how much I'm dying to feel your hands on me."

Babe. No one had ever called her that. She suspected she should be insulted by it, as a modern, independent woman. But she wasn't. Especially not when he'd also admitted his blatant need in that thick, hungry tone.

"I want to spend the night inside your tight little body, not a hospital emergency room."

"Wow," she muttered, collapsing into her seat. Blunt he may be, but the man *definitely* knew how to use words to their best effect.

"You okay?"

Voiceless, she merely nodded.

One of her hands remained on his leg, covered by his. Jake slowly lifted it to his lips. Pressing a soft kiss on her fingers, he said, "I'll make it up to you. I plan to make you feel incredible all night long."

All night long. Oh, goodness. His tone had been sultry and full of promise. Her whole body was already on edge, thrumming and alive from that crazy-hot encounter outside the pub. Now, with his sweet whisper washing over her, she went almost gooey with want.

But not so gooey that she didn't realize she had one remaining coherent brain cell, which hissed a final word of caution in her ear. *Unsafe*, he'd said. He wouldn't do something unsafe.

God, she hadn't even thought about the safe sex aspect of this crazy, impulsive decision. She, who thought her way around every problem at least a dozen times before committing to a response, had skipped right past the inherent dangers of his profession. She'd agreed to let a man who had sex for money pleasure her all night long, without a thought of her own physical well-being until now.

How did one handle this type of situation? It wasn't as if she'd ever encountered it, or heard of a guidebook describing how someone made sure a hired lover wasn't carrying around any nasty reminders of previous *clients*.

Then she thought about it. Oliver had cheated on her, not only with the snow ho, but with many others. Or so she'd heard after they broke up.

She knew guys who'd had sex with dozens of girls in high school and college. Sometimes they even proudly offered different colored bracelets to the girls they scored with, so the easier ones could advertise just how far they were willing to go—and thereby get more dates. More meaningless sexual partners.

Just because *she* had only ever had a half-dozen or so lovers didn't mean everyone else in her circle had. Many, she suspected, probably had as much experience as a pro like Jake did. Some even more.

Her sister included.

So she decided to treat him as she would any other potential lover. *Openly.*

"We have to use protection. I have condoms at my place."

His eyes widened and he glanced over at her, his handsome face—hard-planed, masculine, magnificent—spotlighted by the headlights of cars in the distance.

"I mean, it's not that I don't trust you. But in this day and age…"

"I'm not offended."

Thank goodness.

He returned his focus to the road. "Just so we're clear, I'm also not hiding any unpleasant conditions. I have to get routine physicals, it's part of the job, and I am entirely healthy."

She didn't really want to talk about his job, or even think about it. *This is personal*, she reminded herself. So she simply replied, "Great." Then, since fair was fair, added, "For the record, I'm absolutely fine, too."

He grinned and winked, breaking the awkward moment. "Yes, indeed, you are, Ms. Turner. Absolutely *fine*."

Then there was nothing left. No barriers. No excuses. No doubts. They'd reached her building and he was pulling into her private parking space in the underground garage. Their next stop would be the elevator, and then her penthouse apartment.

After that, a night in the arms of the kind of lover women competed for. Dreamed about.

And for this one night, he was entirely hers.

6

THOUGH HE RECOGNIZED the exclusive high-rise building, and had been warned by Maddy's comments about her bed and her bathtub, Jake hadn't really been prepared for the opulence of her home.

First of all, only in movies had he ever seen keyed elevators that opened directly into private apartments. He didn't think they actually existed.

Not that he'd really been paying attention until the doors had quietly swished open with a subdued ding. Because from the moment they'd gotten into the elevator down in the garage, he'd had his hand on Maddy's soft ass and his mouth on the side of her neck.

The scent of her warm brown hair and her sweet skin had intoxicated him and he'd been unable to resist moving behind her, grinding into her, reaching around to press his hand onto her stomach and pull her hard against him.

They'd *both* been distracted then. She'd lifted her arm behind her to drape it around his neck, holding him in place. Arching back against his erection, she'd groaned with a kind of raw, primal pleasure that told him she might just like this particular position with her clothes *off.*

Mmm.

That could definitely be arranged, though not until he'd had her face-to-face, breath-to-breath first. He wanted to watch her eyes as he slowly sank into her, wanted to feel her gasps, hear the little hitch in her throat as she whimpered at how good it felt.

After that…well, he couldn't even begin to list the ways he wanted this woman.

He'd envisioned most of them on the way up. Then they'd reached her floor, the doors had opened, and he felt as though he'd stepped into a designer furniture store where Oprah shopped up on the Magnificent Mile.

The entryway was tiled with what he'd speculate was Italian marble, not that he'd ever seen it. But he doubted they'd allow the fake stuff in this building.

Tall, graceful vases with a profusion of perfectly placed, enormous white flowers stood on either side of the foyer, providing an almost snowy, winter welcome. Right in the middle of June.

Beyond lay a plushly carpeted, sunken living area. More vases and flowers stood sentry throughout. Big, gold-leaf framed mirrors sent his own reflection back to him a dozen times. Several pieces of expensive-looking, froufrou art were on display, discreetly placed fixtures flooding them with light from just the right angle.

A huge white leather sofa looked too pristine to sit on, and he'd probably have to sell his truck to replace the marble-topped coffee table if he dared leave a drink ring on it.

The place was unbelievably elegant. Dripping with expensive furnishings. Beautiful. Rich-looking.

And about as cold a room as he'd ever seen.

Entirely suitable for the ice princess of the financial district. But not for the woman who'd grabbed him by the shirt and shoved him up against the wall outside that pub to kiss the lips right off his face.

Maddy was watching him, having stepped inside ahead of him to punch a few buttons on a security alarm panel. There was a glimmer of hesitation in her expression, as if she really cared what he thought about her home. *Why* she'd care about the opinion of a blue-collar rescue worker, whose single piece of art in his apartment was an eight-by-ten framed picture of a Dalmatian on a fire truck, he had no idea.

"Well?"

"Wow."

She wrapped her arms around her waist and stared at the room, obviously noting his unenthusiastic response. "My sister decorated it for me," she whispered. "I just don't have the knack for that sort of thing. Or the vision."

That figured. From what he'd heard so far, he had absolutely no interest in ever meeting the sister. Especially not if she envisioned *this* when she looked at Maddy, whom she obviously did not really know at all.

"Great view," he mumbled, meaning that. She did have an amazing view of the magnificently lit Chicago skyline. One entire wall of windows ran the width of the living room, laying out the city below as if he was looking at a galaxy of stars from above.

She perked up, smiling broadly. "Isn't it? That's why I bought it. Well, that and the bathroom."

Bought it. She *owned* this icy masterpiece. Not her father, not her family. She didn't just rent it. The woman he'd taken out for wings and beer had enough money to actually *purchase* a place like this.

He'd known that. Logically, he'd known. Still, the meaning of it had at last completely sunk in.

His feet suddenly felt leaden. For the first time since the moment they'd met, Jake felt the slightest bit intimidated. Uneasy at the stark, irrefutable evidence of how different they were.

There was no way he could keep up with this. Nor would he ever even want to try.

"What's wrong?"

He threw off the momentary uneasiness. Tomorrow, maybe he'd think about how unsuited they were for one another. Tonight, well, they were perfectly suited in the only way that *really* mattered. He'd could definitely keep up with her in other ways.

Starting in her bedroom.

"Nothing." He gave her a wolfish smile. "So where is this three-man bathtub?"

"Hey, none of that kinky stuff," she reminded him with a saucy wink. Then she turned and sashayed down the hall, kicking her cute, strappy sandals off her feet midstride, as if not wanting to waste time once they reached the bed.

He followed, not in any hurry, because they had all night, but still unable to stop himself from lifting his shirt over his head and tossing it to the floor with her shoes.

She led him into a darkened room, flipped on the light, and spun around to gauge his reaction. But when she saw him standing there in just his soft, low-slung jeans, she froze as if she'd never seen a man's body before.

"Oh, my God."

The sexy woman actually licked her lips while her gaze greedily roamed over his bare chest and shoulders. She looked even hungrier than she had when their waitress had deposited a pile of nachos in front of her tonight.

"I never imagined," she whispered, lifting her hand toward him. She didn't step closer, merely scraping the tip of one finger down his throat, until reaching the hollow of his throat. There it remained, connected by the tiniest strand of static-charged air to his raging pulse. "I've never seen a more beautiful man."

Jake half groaned and half laughed.

"I mean it. You're beautiful. You should be on display somewhere, dipped in bronze. You're so hard, so strong." She ran her hand down his chest, letting her pink-tinged nails rake lightly across his abs. She didn't pause, caressing him until she reached the waistband of his jeans, which hung low on his hips. Visibly swallowing, she added, "Yet so lean, too."

"You're killing me. You know this, right?"

She ignored him. "I'd pictured…when I went to the auction, I'd figured you'd be skinny. Elegant. Not…not like *this*."

He barked a harsh laugh. Skinny he was not. And elegant he'd never tried to be. "I work out sometimes. Not out of vanity, out of necessity."

There was no way Jake would put somebody's life at risk by letting himself get too out of shape to do his job. He lifted gurneys—usually with heavy bodies on them—every single day. He squeezed into small spaces in collapsed buildings, he often hauled around some backbreakingly heavy equipment. Those things mattered—possibly enough to be the difference between life and death to an injured person. Staying in top physical condition was an absolute requirement for his own safety and for that of others.

"Is it a necessity that your shoulders are as broad as my legs are long?"

He chuckled, glancing down at those delicate, sexy legs, in such perfect proportion to the rest of her, despite her claim that they were too short. "I think that's a bit of an exaggeration." Then he reached for her hips, cupped them and drew her close. "But I'm willing to examine them, up close and personal, just to make sure."

"I'd hate to ask such a sacrifice of you."

"What can I say? I'm a nice guy."

Maddy, who'd been inching closer as they engaged in the light, verbal foreplay, tilted her head back and watched him intently. "You are, aren't you."

"You make it sound like it's a bad thing."

She shook her head. "You're a contradiction, that's all. I don't know that I understand you."

"Understand this." He said nothing more, bending down to cover her mouth with his. Slipping his hands into her hair to cup her head, he licked her lips, demanding access.

Maddy opened for him, her tongue meeting with his in a

warm, slow exploration. Different from the crazy-hot kiss outside the pub. Different…but just as good.

Their bodies melted together in fluid grace, rather than heated, crazed grinding. Her softness cradled every hard place on him, molding to his chest, his groin, his thighs. Every delicate curve offered warmth and welcome and pure feminine invitation.

"Jake…" she whispered against his mouth, though he knew she had nothing to say. Nothing that really needed to be said.

They'd talked a lot since they'd met. Now it was time for their bodies to do all the communicating.

Reaching for the bottom of her pink top, Jake tugged it free of her waistband, sliding it up with agonizing restraint. He didn't look, didn't trust himself to *see* her yet and not completely lose control. He concentrated instead on kissing her temple, tracing her high cheekbone with his mouth, kissing his way to the lobe of her ear. And continuing to pull that fabric up, inch by inch, allowing only the tips of his fingers the pleasure of contact with her warm, soft skin.

She was gasping, her choppy breaths hitting his neck as she twisted against his hands. "Please."

"Mmm, hmm," he replied, not giving her the frenzy she wanted. She might have been calling the shots back outside the pub. But for now, their first time, he was taking control.

He liked it slow. And intended to make her slow down, too. He wanted Maddy to accept every ounce of pleasure he could give her rather than rushing them both directly toward that precipice and leaping over it.

"You have the softest skin I have ever felt," he murmured.

"Yours is rough," she whispered, her voice throaty, hungry. Rubbing her face against his lightly grizzled jaw, she shivered and added, "Deliciously rough."

"Not too rough for your cheek?"

She shook her head, wordless, mindless, as if afraid to distract him from the unhurried, steady progress he was making with her shirt. He'd reached the bottom edges of her bra now. Remembering their earlier encounter, his mind flooded with the image of that hot pink lace barely covering those magnificent mounds and luscious, taut nipples.

"Not too rough for your neck, either?" He moved there, kissing his way down her throat, pressing his mouth to the hollow.

She shook her head again. Lifting her hands to his head, she twined her fingers in his hair. Jake edged away just enough to smooth her top all the way up, his palms skimming against the sides of her breasts, then all the way along her upraised arms. He disentangled the fabric from her long, thick hair, then tossed it aside.

Looking down at her, he muttered a silent prayer for strength, picturing the endless ways he wanted to savor these twin things of beauty, barely contained by their lacy covering. Oh, *so* many ways. *Soon.*

"What about here?" he asked, easing down her body. "Too rough here, sweetheart?" He slowly dropped to his knees in front of her, letting his mouth skim past the very center of the pretty, frilly bra until he reached the vulnerable skin of her midriff.

She hitched a sigh. It turned into a moan when Jake rubbed his cheek there, licking at the tender, pale spot where hot pink lace met hot creamy woman.

"That's…that's fine…"

"Good. So I'm guessing this is okay, too." He edged lower, kissing his way down her belly, dipping his tongue into the small indentation for a taste, then going down to her waistband. She made no effort to stop him as he unbuttoned, unzipped, then pushed her pants down, letting his cheek come in contact with more of her body as it was revealed.

"That is *definitely* okay."

More than okay for him. Especially as he drew back enough to watch her cropped pants fall away. That left her clad in a miniscule pair of panties. A patch of pink fabric danced over the dark curls he saw shadowed between her legs, and a thin, lacy string looped over each full hip.

He rubbed and nibbled and licked his way along them, around to her hip, almost groaning as he saw how little there was in the back. Little? Make that nothing.

Thong. Oh yeah.

He had to reach out and touch with his hands, cupping her full cheeks and squeezing. "Incredible. Don't you *ever* let me hear you say you want to change this body again."

The way her legs shook and her hips moved in tiny, nearly imperceptible thrusts told him what she wanted. More intimate touches. More intimate kisses.

More.

Still clasping her bottom, he tugged her closer, tilting her pelvis so his mouth scraped against the front of her panties. He inhaled her, breathed across her, amazed at the softness of the curls against his lips, looking delicate and so pretty, even through the fabric.

"Oh, God, please," she groaned.

He could give her what she wanted. Could easily nudge aside the elastic, dip his tongue, swirl it low. Could already imagine the way she'd writhe when he caressed the throbbing nub of flesh at the top of her mound. Could almost taste the warm, womanly essence he was inhaling with every deep breath. He desperately wanted to lick into the lips of her sex and drink deeply of her, knowing it would take a long time to quench his thirst.

But that would be getting ahead of the game.

So, instead, he began working his way back up. "Now that we're sure I don't need to shave, where were we?"

She whimpered, shaking as he passed by her most erogenous

spots. "I take it back, you're not a nice guy," she said in a broken whisper. "You're just being mean now."

"Oh, Maddy, I'm not mean." Now standing directly in front of her, he tenderly stroked her face and brushed a soft kiss on her mouth. "I'm just very, *very* patient."

Without another word, he bent over and picked her up, carrying her effortlessly to the huge bed that dominated her room. And began to show her how very patient he could be.

MADDY WAS DYING. And living. Flying. Spinning. Both crying in frustration and shouting in pure delight as she climaxed again and again. Over the next hour, as Jake—with his incredible mouth, his miraculous hands—continued to touch, kiss, taste every inch of her body, she found herself unable to do a single thing but enjoy it.

Rational thoughts drifted away. There was only sensation. No decision to arch up when his tongue scraped across her nipple, just a primal need to have him suckle her again. No conscious awareness that he intended to make the most intimate love to her with his mouth, just the shocking delight of it when his tongue slipped between her wet folds and unerringly delved into her core.

"Oh, God, again?" she groaned, disbelieving as the pressure built, then roared into heat that rushed to every other part of her.

She had not known she was physically capable of such continuous delight. The waves kept coming, relentlessly, like the pounding of the surf on a shore during a wild winter storm. They built, took her high, threw her over the crest into wild orgasm. Then eased back down, only to start building all over again with a stroke here or a kiss there.

She understood now. Why women fought over him.

The man had to be the world's greatest lover.

"I think I have to be in you now, Maddy."

"I'd say it's about damn time," she gasped. "But I'd be lying if I didn't admit I've loved every single minute."

"I know." No cockiness. Just pure, sultry self-confidence.

He slid up her body, finally unfastening his jeans and pushing them off his hips as he moved over her. She kissed him, licking into his mouth, tasting herself on his tongue but not giving a damn.

But she was not about to let him sheathe himself with one of the condoms she'd grabbed from the bedside table without at least a little reciprocation. Maddy had been dying to experience some of what he'd done. To touch, to stroke, to *see* him at the very least. He had ruthlessly stopped her every previous effort to do so in his determination to please her.

Now, the incredible willpower seemed to have finally left him. He was almost beyond rational thought, too.

Maddy pushed him onto his back, rolling up to kneel beside him, staring at the immense golden chest, the wiry hair surrounding his nipples. It trailed in a thin line down his flat stomach, disappearing beneath the waistband of his tight boxer briefs.

"Oh my," she whispered, seeing the big bulge in the middle of those briefs. She'd certainly felt the power of him pressed against her, but her eyes hadn't yet experienced the pleasure. Nor had her hands. Or her mouth.

That was about to change.

She reached out, tentatively, touching a spot of wetness on the fabric. Almost dazed with need, she brought her finger to her tongue and tasted it.

"Maddy..."

"I don't want to hear one word out of you," she warned sternly. "Not a single word."

"Yes, ma'am." Laughter danced in his eyes, but didn't spill from his mouth. No, his mouth was too busy emitting a deep, guttural groan as Maddy reached down and tugged at the briefs.

She was careful, cautious when pulling them out and down.

Maddy wanted that magnificent erection revealed to her as deliberately, slowly and seductively as her breasts had been to him. As if she was opening some very special, beautifully wrapped present that was going to make her incredibly happy.

Well, wasn't she?

Her hand shook as the side of her pinky brushed against the smooth, incredibly soft skin beneath the cotton. Some anticipatory devil made her close her eyes, wanting to delay the delicious moment of exposure.

When she'd finally pulled the boxers all the way to his hips, Jake lifted up a little and pushed them down and off himself.

And Maddy finally opened her eyes.

"Oh, Jake," she whispered, unable to contain a tiny gasp of surprise. Not just because of how incredibly hard—aroused, throbbing and proud—he was, but at the pure masculine beauty of him. Still kneeling at his hip, she smiled—almost purred, really—as she stared greedily at the velvet-skinned member.

Her last lover had been incredibly long and thin *there*, believing his extreme length made any kind of skill unnecessary.

Jake, well, he was something else *entirely*. He might not have the inordinate length, but she should have expected, given the breadth of his shoulders and chest, that the man would be unbelievably thick in other places, too.

My God.

Soon he'd be doing exactly as he'd promised earlier—filling her so completely she'd wonder if she was going to break in half.

They seemed to have skipped past the basics of a new sexual relationship, as Maddy understood them. Which meant she didn't have to wait until the second or third time they slept together to do what she was just dying to do. Reaching out, she stroked him, one long caress along the back of his erection, then delicately touched the taut sacs beneath.

He hissed. She remained undeterred. Spreading her hand

wide, she encircled as much of him as she could, then slowly moved closer, her mouth going wet with hunger.

"Maddy!"

"Not a word," she reminded him.

Then there was no more talking, just the sensation of her lips sliding over the smooth round head, her tongue moistening him enough so she could take a little more. And a little more after that.

Not oblivious to his clenched fists or the rock-hard muscles in his stomach, that said he was fighting very hard to remain in control, Maddy showed no mercy.

She liked how he tasted. She liked how he felt in her mouth. She liked the scrape of his hard-yet-soft flesh against the insides of her cheeks, and the tiny groan he made when she took him all the way, as deep as he could possibly go.

That was when he lost it.

Without another word, Jake pushed her away. He grabbed her by the shoulders and yanked her up, flipping her on her back so fast, she didn't even have time to process the change in position.

"Uh-uh. I don't think so."

Maddy put on an intentional pout, liking that she'd driven him to such desperation. "But I was having fun."

"You can have more of that kind of fun later. I'm not coming in your mouth. I want to do it inside your body."

"My mouth's part of my body…"

He thrust a thick, hard finger into her dripping sex, making her gasp and arch hard against his hand. "*Here.* I want to be here." Another finger joined it, and he moved them in and out, slowly making love to her…preparing her. "Right now, I think I need to be inside you more than I need to live until my thirtieth birthday."

Wrapping her arms around his neck, she murmured, "Well, we can't have you not surviving your twenties."

Jake kissed her, hard and deep, then grabbed the condom which he'd already torn open. She reached to help him, but he pushed her hand away. "Don't push me, babe, I'm holding on by a thread."

"Does that mean it's going to be over really quickly?" she asked, unable to hide a hint of worry.

Rather than take offense, Jake threw his head back and laughed. "Hell, no. It means that once I'm in you, you can't torment me anymore."

"Torment you?" She arched a brow. "Was that what I was doing?"

"Yeah, babe, it was, and you know it. You were trying to drive me wild, and oh, it was definitely working."

Good.

"And being inside you is *also* going to drive me wild," he admitted. "But there, at least, I can stay very still." His whiskey tone promised incredible delights, seducing her word by word. "I can indulge in the feel of you wrapped around me. Not moving, just savoring."

"Not moving?" The idea of trying to remain still when *that* was inside her was beyond comprehension.

"Not a muscle," he growled. "Not until I feel capable of *really* getting started."

Getting started. Oh, my. As if she hadn't already had more orgasms in the past hour than she'd had during her entire relationship with her ex.

He pushed her legs apart—far enough apart to accommodate the breadth of him, and Maddy arched up, opening herself in welcome. Maybe a teeny, tiny bit tentative.

As if knowing, Jake kissed her tenderly, whispering soft words against her mouth that relaxed her, telling her he'd never do anything to hurt her.

Slowly, with more of that unbelievable restraint he seemed to have by the barrel, he eased into her. Just the tip of his heat, then an inch more, and even more after that. Until, finally, he plunged deep, drawing a deep, guttural gasp from both of them.

Just as he'd promised, he filled her completely.

She whimpered, needing to move, overwhelmed by how damn *good* it felt. Her muscles reacted, squeezed, milked him deep inside.

"Wait," he growled.

"I'm not moving," she protested in her own defense.

"The hell you're not."

She squeezed again, helpless against her body's instinctive response.

This time, he didn't order her to stop, he merely distracted her by lowering a hand between them. Tweaking and toying with her throbbing clit, he brought all her focus there. Filled by him, covered by him, touched by him, everything came together once more and within moments he had her crying out as she came again.

"Mmm," he groaned, his eyes closed, obviously feeling the involuntary clench of every muscle she had.

Finally, when she'd begun to feel somewhat sane again, Jake pulled out, slowly, slid back, just as slowly, going a little deeper, stretching her a little wider, driving her out of what was left of her mind.

"Now, Maddy," he whispered hoarsely, sounding as if he was finally letting himself go completely, "now we're getting started."

7

JAKE WOULD HAVE LOVED nothing more than to spend a whole day in bed with Maddy. But very early the next morning, after a full night of the most intense lovemaking of his life, he glanced at the clock by her bed and knew he had to go. His shift started in two hours and he still had to flag down a cab to get him back to the lot where he'd left his truck. Then he'd need to rush home, shower and grab his gear.

Besides, Maddy had already taken yesterday afternoon off for the game. He doubted he could cajole another day of hooky from work out of the woman, despite how desperately she needed one.

He hated to wake her, but he certainly wasn't going to leave without saying goodbye. Knowing he shouldn't delay, he still couldn't force himself to do anything but watch her sleep for just a little while longer.

Maddy's long lashes rested on her cheeks, her beautiful, kiss-reddened lips were parted as she drew in slow, even breaths. The sun had begun to rise, glints of light appearing on the horizon laid out beyond the floor-to-ceiling windows of her bedroom. As he watched her slumber, long rays of brilliant golden sunshine gradually traveled across the room, falling onto the bed. It caught the highlights in her hair and spotlighted her beautiful face.

No ice queen this. She looked as warm and sensual as a summer angel.

"Maddy?" he whispered, leaning over to brush a soft kiss on the corner of her mouth. "I've got to go."

She went from a deep sleep to full wakefulness in an instant, her eyes flying open. Staring at the ceiling, he could almost see the wheels churning in her brain as she put together the memories of all the wild and wicked things they'd done together the night before.

Finally, licking her lips, she turned her head to look at him. "Jake."

"Expecting somebody else?" he asked with a laugh.

He bent to kiss her good-morning, but Maddy slipped away before he could do it. She scooted to the edge of the bed, stood, then glanced down at her naked body.

She wore nothing but sunlight *very* well.

Unfortunately, she didn't wear it for long. Grabbing a silky robe from her dresser, she yanked it on. She tied the sash tightly around her waist, crossed her arms and clenched the fabric in her fists, still not sparing him a glance.

Maddy was obviously suffering a case of morning-after embarrassment. For that reason, he didn't have the heart to tease her about covering up what he'd seen a whole lot of the night before.

Finally she spoke. "I, uh, have to get ready for work." Gesturing toward the hallway, she added, "There's another bathroom right down the hall, if you'd like to take a shower, too."

Jake frowned, realizing this wasn't just a case of misplaced shyness. Maddy was trying desperately to get everything back under control, to put her life back in its natural order. She'd surrendered that control—in fact, allowed some serious *dis*order— last night, giving herself over to him, body and mind. Now, in the clear light of morning, she wanted it back.

All of it.

"I'll take one at home," he murmured, honestly not knowing

how to proceed. For the first time since he'd met her, he was at a loss as to how to deal with this woman.

Then he remembered his parents, grandparents and all the other successful couples he'd ever known. They had one thing in common—the ability to give and take. To be in charge, and to step back. Ebb and flow.

He'd had his way last night. Maybe it was time to let her have hers, even if it meant allowing her to start building those barriers around herself once more.

He could get past them again. Last night had proved it.

Suddenly appearing stricken, Maddy said, "Oh, I just remembered, we left your truck…"

"It's not a problem. I'll hail a cab to take me over to the lot." He wondered for a second if she'd tell him not to bother.

She didn't.

Okay. Interlude definitely over. Time to get out, let her get her head together and start planning for next time.

"When can I see you again?"

She clenched the robe tighter. "Again?"

"Never heard of a second date?"

"Ours wasn't exactly a typical first one for me."

He couldn't prevent a confident smile. "I sure hope not."

Maddy's chin went up. "Was it for *you?*"

He didn't even hesitate. "Not a chance. Last night was…well, something I never expected. But it's something I'm very thankful for." Glancing at the clock, he muttered a curse and hunted around on the floor for his clothes. "I really do have to go, though. There are people counting on me."

He found his things and began to dress, finally looking back at her, to see her frozen in the same spot, her face pale, her eyes narrowed, as if she'd been glaring at him behind his back. "Are you mad about something?" he asked, dropping his jeans and stepping closer.

"No. Don't be silly. The sun's a little blinding, that's all." She cleared her throat. "Go on, finish dressing, we've both got places to be."

Something was seriously wrong. And if he hadn't already played on his lieutenant's mercy to get a schedule change yesterday to attend the game, he'd seriously consider trying to find someone to cover for him. As it was, he didn't have that option. Ninety minutes left. Damn.

He stepped into the jeans, yanking them up. "Let's get together…day after tomorrow?"

"You're busy until then, I assume?" Talk about icy-toned.

"Yeah. Booked solid for the next forty-eight hours." He had a twenty-four-hour shift, then a twelve, with on-call time in between. The last thing he wanted was to get busy doing something incredible with this woman and get called out, having to leave her high and dry. And him high and *hard*.

"I see."

"I'll take you to dinner." Suddenly remembering what had happened at the pub, Jake reached into his back pocket and pulled out his wallet. "Speaking of which, I need to pay you back for last night. Some gentleman I am."

She waved an airy hand. "Don't be ridiculous."

"I'm not some macho he-man, okay?" he said, "But you shelled out twenty-five thousand dollars and the least I can do is cover some wings and beer."

Maddy's smile was tight and it did not soften her beautiful brown eyes one bit. "That wasn't the *least* you could do. You did a whole lot more than that last night for my twenty-five thousand dollars. So let's call it even."

It took him a second to catch her meaning, and when he did, Jake couldn't stop a half-amused, half-annoyed grunt. "Uh, it's flattering that you think I might be worth it, but you didn't pay me all that money so I'd spend last night in your bed."

"No, I paid a charity."

For a night in bed with him. She didn't say it. The implication was clear.

He chalked up her belligerence to her own uncertainty and didn't call her on the fact that she'd just backhandedly called him a male prostitute. "You're being ridiculous."

"Why *did* you spend last night in my bed?"

Yeesh, the woman had some seriously selective memory. Good thing he suspected she was worth this much effort. "Because, as I already told you, I *wanted* you. Period. End of story." *And I still do.*

"Okay." Nodding and lifting her chin, she admitted, "I wanted you, too. But now that's over, and I really think we should quit while we're ahead."

His jaw dropped. "What?"

"Last night was lovely, Jake. But I don't think we'll be seeing each other again."

He had had enough of giving Maddy her space. Walking the few feet it took to get to her, he took her chin in his hand, forcing her to look at him. "What the hell is wrong?"

She jerked away. "Nothing's wrong. I just can't deal with this. With the…difficulties of this situation. So we need to end it here and now." Finally uncrossing her arms, she ran a weary hand over her eyes. "I can't imagine seeing you under…*professional* circumstances."

"Well, Jesus, I hope not. I don't want to see you hurt."

"Thank you," she murmured. Then she stiffened again. "But I can't see you personally, either. Because, as much as I might *say* I'm modern and hip and can handle anything, that would end up bothering me, too."

There was that pessimistic streak. He'd been wondering when it would return. The woman had been covered by it for so long, he was surprised she'd been able to get out from under the weight of her disdain for romance long enough to go to bed with him.

"Goodbye, Jake," she said, not even giving him a chance to respond. Instead, she spun around, walked into her bathroom and shut the door firmly behind her.

Give it up. Come back for round three.

But he didn't listen to the voice in his head. Not this time. Instead, he finished dressing, put on his boots, then knocked on the bathroom door. "I'm leaving now. But I want you to know, this isn't over."

Hearing the shower go on inside, he knocked harder. "Damn it, Maddy, at least tell me you'll talk to me about this in a few days."

She didn't come out. But she did answer. And what she said shocked Jake so much he couldn't make his brain work for several long seconds.

"No. I can't do it. Once was enough. I can't go to bed with you again, wondering whose bed you just left, and how much she paid you to be there."

Paid him?

"I'm not criticizing you for the way you live, but frankly, Jake, I can't afford you. Financially, yes. Emotionally, however, I don't have that kind of currency to spend. Now please leave."

He stared at the door, his jaw falling open, staggering back into her room until his legs hit the bed. He collapsed onto it, still stunned.

The woman thought he had sex for money. Despite what he'd said about wanting her from first sight, she truly believed he'd spent last night here as some kind of sick, twisted payoff for the cash she'd shelled out at the auction. She'd completely ignored everything he'd said, everything they'd shared. She hadn't trusted that he'd actually felt something real and genuine for her.

"What the hell kind of world do you live in, lady?" he muttered under his breath, still staring at the closed door. Then he glanced around the room—done in white and silver—cold and icy like the rest of the place. And remembered the kind of world she lived in.

One where anything could be bought for a price…including people, including sex. Where love didn't exist, or at least, didn't last.

One that absolutely had no place for somebody like him.

"CAN YOU PLEASE explain this to me? You had the best night of your life with a dreamboat of a man who could give lessons to the god of love, and you told him you never wanted to see him again. Does that about sum it up?"

Maddy cast a quick glance around the quiet, upscale restaurant a few blocks from the bank. It was empty except for a few late-lunch–early-Friday-happy-hour patrons, none of whom, fortunately, appeared to have overheard Tabitha's way-too-personal observation.

She still glared at her sister, who, as usual, was impeccably dressed, perfectly groomed, not an ash-blond hair out of place. And looking every bit as put-together as Maddy felt torn apart.

"Yes. That sums it up very well, to me and every other person in the place."

Tabby rolled her eyes, entirely unrepentant. "I think the stork mixed you up with a nun's baby at birth." The incongruity of that statement didn't seem to occur to her older sibling, who shook her head, reached into her expensive purse and retrieved a jeweled cigarette case. "You're just too demure to be my sister."

"Uh, madam?" a voice said from beside the table. The obsequious maître d' had appeared like a vapor. "I'm afraid you cannot smoke here."

Tabby audibly growled, put the case away and muttered, "Nazi," behind the retreating man's stiff back. "Can't smoke around Bradley, can't smoke in public…." Then she snapped her long, red-tinted nails against the pristine white tablecloth, tapping out a beat in visible irritation. "Tell me why not."

"Why can't you smoke? Aside from it being horribly unhealthy, and—"

"Why you can't be with him," Tabby growled, not fooled one bit. And she was even more pissy now that she couldn't light up.

Maddy started with the obvious. "Well, he *is* a prostitute."

"So? You're telling me most of the women we know haven't essentially prostituted themselves by trading sex for the right size diamond on their finger?"

"You included?" Maddy asked, hoping her sister was not marrying for the wrong reason. Again.

"Money has nothing to do with why I'm marrying Bradley." Tabitha's tone was sharp. "I love him. Besides, you and I both know I don't need his money, and he doesn't need mine."

That was one reason Maddy had high hopes for her sister's next marriage. There was no obvious reason—beyond compatibility and real emotion—for the couple to wed. "True."

"The point is, people trade commodities all the time. Money for property. Stocks for liquid assets. Sex for marriage. Look at my mother—off on some yacht in the Mediterranean with her latest. Do you know she's not even coming home for the wedding?"

Having met Tabitha's mother more than a few times while growing up, Maddy could muster no surprise. Sympathy, yes. But no surprise.

"Anyway," Tabitha continued, returning to the subject at hand, far beyond any ability to be hurt by her neglectful mother. "Why not a hot affair for a few bucks?"

She tried to put it in perspective for her sister. "Have you noticed that I've never bought a used car?"

"As if you'd need to," Tabitha replied, not getting the point.

Remaining patient, Maddy bit out, "I don't particularly care to take another nighttime spin with someone who's piling on the mileage with other drivers during the day."

"Ahh, I get it. That is a little, um, distasteful," Tabitha admitted. Grimacing, she continued. "Imagine if Bitsy Wellington or one of those old collagen-injected, stapled-together wicked witches tracked him down."

Thank God her sister hadn't mentioned their stepmother's name. That mental image was enough to make Maddy nauseous.

"But certainly you're not naive enough to think men don't sleep around." Squinting her nose in disgust, Tabitha added, "You certainly should have learned that much from that bastard Oliver."

"I did. But it's not just the physical squeamishness. I actually like Jake. Maybe I like him too much," Maddy admitted, angry both at herself for voicing the words, and at Tabby for making her.

"Oh." Her sister's expression softened. "I see."

Maddy believed she did.

"It's not the ick factor. It would be too *emotionally* painful to be with him one day," Tabitha mused, "knowing he might have been with someone else the night before."

Exactly. Painful. Uncomfortable. Too much to take.

Maddy was a strong woman, but she was not *that* strong. She had already developed feelings for Jake in the brief time they'd spent together. *Friendly feelings*, she forced herself to remember. *Just* friendly.

Well, and lustful ones, she had to concede.

But with just those—*friendly* feelings—it had still horrified her to think of him leaving her home Wednesday morning to go spend forty-eight hours with another woman due to a previous booking.

How much worse it might be if she continued to see him, she couldn't imagine. Which was why she was still certain she'd made the right decision in sending him away. Even if, at least physically, she'd been regretting it ever since.

Her mind had been one hundred percent responsible for the plan. But her body was still pretty unhappy about it.

"Maybe he'd give it up for you."

"Don't be ridiculous. Why should he? He's known me for less than ten days."

Tabitha pursed her lips slightly, then lifted her hand and rubbed her chin. Maddy recognized the look. It was what got her into this mess in the first place. "No."

"No what?"

"No to whatever scheme you've come up with."

"You wound me."

"You have dragon scales in place of skin, Tab. You can't be wounded."

"I can if I'm struck through the heart." That should have come across as earnest and sincere, but Maddy knew her sister well enough to hear the note of jaded amusement.

"Well, I don't have scales or protective armor around *my* heart, either. So I'm not risking it." *Not now. Not ever again.*

"Think of it logically—what would you be risking if you got involved with him *physically*?"

"Uh, humiliation, jealousy, venereal disease?"

Tabby shuddered lightly. "You *did* use…"

"Of course. And he assured me he's fine. I imagine anybody with a lot of partners keeps on top of that sort of thing in this day and age."

"Why do you think I have my gynecologist on speed dial?"

"Too much 4-1-1."

Tabby thankfully got back to the point. "But those things wouldn't be an issue if he wasn't seeing anybody else."

"We've been over this already. I'm not going to ask a man I've known for less than two weeks to change his whole life for me."

Not only because it was too much to ask, but because she already knew he'd say no. Any reasonable person would resist a major life change like that this early in a relationship. Unless they were really—*really*—head over heels in love.

Which didn't describe her and Jake Wallace.

Legs over shoulders in lust? Absolutely. But nothing more. Not a chance.

"So don't ask him to change a thing." Tabitha reached for her wineglass and smiled like the proverbial Cheshire chat. "Just hire him full-time."

Maddy had taken a sip of her own, but Tabby's comment nearly made her spew it out. "What?" Noting the attention her yelped response had garnered, she leaned over the table and kept her voice low. "Are you insane?"

"Are you telling me you can't afford it? Come on, you have the money. Call him up, ask him how much he'd charge to be exclusive for, say, one month."

Exclusive.

"Then take that month and use it to see what happens. You either get him out of your system, or you find out the two of you really can develop something meaningful."

"Meaningful enough to…"

Tabby finished the thought. "To see if he'd be willing to make a permanent *career* change." Her sister reached across the table, covering Maddy's hand and squeezing it gently, with tenderness that always lurked beneath the surface but was so rarely shown. "And to see if you can finally let yourself believe in love again."

"Love," Maddy said with a snort. That wasn't even part of this whole situation. She'd said she *liked* Jake, not that she was falling in love with him. She wasn't *ever* going to fall in love with anyone again. Everyone else in her family had that emotion well taken care of.

Lust…well, lust she could handle. And liking. And maybe some more of the fun she sensed she could have with Jake Wallace. As for the rest—him quitting his "career" for her? Crazy. Madness. Absolutely out of the question.

But for some reason, during the drive home and the long night that followed, Maddy could not get her sister's suggestion out of her mind. And she was still considering it when she woke up the next day.

IT HAD BEEN THREE FULL DAYS and Jake still hadn't quite gotten over his anger—and his confusion—about what had happened with Maddy Wednesday. He'd gone over it again and again. Replayed every moment, every conversation, every look, every touch.

When, he wondered, had she decided he was the kind of man who could be bought?

She had to be jaded beyond belief. Normal people's minds just didn't *go* there for no reason. Which should have been enough to make it easy to live with the fact that they'd never see each other again. But instead, it made him pretty damn angry. Angry—and even sad for her at having become so hard because of her unusual family life.

He was trying determinedly to forget about her. Not successfully, but giving it his best shot. Which was why he'd put his all into this morning's game.

On Saturday mornings, he liked to play baseball with a couple of guys from work. Whoever was off duty met up at a local park—near the station so the on-call guys could join them once in a while.

They'd just finished five innings, with Jake playing third base, before calling it quits because of the already blazing heat of the day and the noon shift change. As he headed toward the benches for his stuff, his cell phone rang. He grabbed it from the side buttoned pocket of his shorts and glanced at the caller ID, but didn't recognize the number.

"Wallace," he barked into it. He tilted his head to hold the phone in the crook of his shoulder while he bagged his stuff and waved to a couple of the guys heading back to the station house.

A feminine throat clearing was the only response at first.

And he'd recognize that feminine throat anywhere.

"Maddy?"

"Yes. Did I interrupt you? I can call back."

"It's fine," he said, wishing he didn't automatically go on full alert at the sound of her voice.

He'd been caught off guard, that was all. He hadn't expected to ever hear from her again. That—and the strenuous game—explained his thudding heart and shortness of breath. Nothing else.

"I wondered if we could meet."

The thudding doubled. Then he focused on her words. *Meet.* Not *go out.*

"Why? You made things pretty clear the other day about where we stood."

"I regret that," she said coolly, sounding not the least bit contrite. The ice queen at her iciest. "And I do apologize."

"Sure."

"I have, however, had a change of heart." Finally her tone faltered, a chink of uncertainty appearing in her fully armored voice. "I may have been a bit too…hasty when I said I didn't want to see you again."

He should tell her to get lost. To take her money, her ice cave disguised as a home and her really twisted assumptions about him and take a hike.

He didn't. Maybe because of that tiny note of uncertainty. Maybe because of the way her hair had looked spread across her pillow in the dawn's first light the other morning. Or the way those dimples flashed every time she genuinely smiled.

He could refuse the ice queen.

But he couldn't refuse the Maddy he'd made love to. The one who was no longer breathing into the phone, as if her breath had been trapped in her lungs and she was holding it close, waiting for his answer. Uncertain. Unsure.

Vulnerable.

"What are you suggesting?"

"I'd like to get together. To…talk things over. I might have a solution to our situation."

"Fine." She breathed again, audibly. And he smiled a little. "We'll talk. We definitely have some things to clear up."

Starting with the whole ridiculous notion she had that he'd slept with her only because she'd put out a whole bunch of money first.

Weren't hookers—male or female—supposed to actually keep *the money they earned?*

He almost laughed at the thought, but didn't. Not while Maddy was still trying to carefully set up a meeting without revealing how anxious she truly was.

He *so* did not get the woman. But he would. Very soon.

"Are you free this afternoon?" she asked.

"I am."

"Wonderful. I, uh…was thinking of taking the boat out. Do you like being on the water?"

The only time he'd been on a boat had been one of those offshore casino ships during a trip to Florida a few years ago. He'd been seasick and had gotten a headache from the constant dings of the slot machines.

"Yeah, love it." *Stupid. She's not going to let her guard down if you're heaving over the side.*

But it was too late. He'd already agreed, and quickly made a note of the location of the boat, docked at the DuSable Harbor marina. He had an hour to get there. Then he'd find out exactly what kind of *solution* Ms. Madeline Turner had for their *situation.*

Jake had one, too. A three-pronged one.

Him telling her she was an idiot to think her money had anything to do with his feelings for her. Her shutting up and believing it. And them getting naked.

Sounded like a great solution to him.

8

MADDY HAD ALREADY BEEN aboard the *Magdalena* when she called Jake on Saturday. The decision to ask him to come with her this afternoon had been an impromptu one. Well, mostly.

She'd intended to call him, having thought all night about her sister's suggestion. At the very least, she wanted to feel him out about the possibility of working "exclusively" for her.

But she hadn't intended to take him out on the water. That had been spontaneous. And also a little sneaky.

It wouldn't be easy for him to laugh in her face and walk away at the very idea if they were a few miles from shore. Not unless he was a really good swimmer.

"My God, I'm turning into my sister," she whispered, knowing Tabitha would approve of the manipulative tactics.

She'd probably also approve of Maddy's attire. Though she hadn't dressed with Jake in mind when she'd made the decision to take the boat out today, she wore a devastatingly skimpy fire-engine red bikini beneath her shorts and tank top.

She usually took the cutter out alone, despite her father's frequent protests. But she was able to handle herself on the lake. And when out there alone, she liked to sunbathe without wearing even as much as that skimpy little bathing suit.

How much fun would it be to do it with someone else?

She'd readied the sails and finished preparations when she saw him walking up the dock toward her. Waving, she called, "I see you found it okay."

"Uh-huh." He gestured toward the side, where *Magdalena* was lovingly painted in large, script letters. "I like the name."

"My mother's," she murmured.

Jake nodded, making no weak, inane, "I'm sorry for your loss" comment like so many people made when they learned she'd lost her mother at such a young age. She liked that about him. One of many things she liked about him.

He looked over the cutter again, from the cabin up to the top of the mast, obviously taken aback by its size. "Do I have to ask for permission to come aboard?"

"You don't have to. Permission *is* granted."

Then he was there, beside her, all tan and masculine, wearing a loose-fitting T-shirt, swim trunks and leather flip-flops. He even had beautiful legs and *feet* for a man.

She didn't know what to say, so she said nothing, waiting for some sign from him. Was he angry? Curious? Optimistic?

When he finally did speak, she realized she hadn't even come close to guessing his mood.

"I'm glad you called," he murmured, tenderly scraping his lips across her temple. "Really glad."

And just like that, with his sweet touch and his sweeter words, she knew she couldn't trick him, couldn't get him out so far that he'd have no choice but to listen to her offer. Nor could she just seduce him into agreement by stripping off her shorts and top and laying herself out like a curvy appetizer.

She had to come clean.

"Jake, I think you already know me enough to realize how difficult this is for me."

"Mmm, hmm." And he wasn't making it any easier, simply waiting for her to continue.

"The thing is," she murmured, smoothing her hands nervously over her white sailor shorts, telling herself she was *not* leaving sweaty palm prints there. "I really would like to spend more time with you."

"Ditto. I'd like to spend more time with you, too."

She smiled, but didn't relax yet. "Only, I *don't* want you spending time with…anyone else."

He tilted a head, confusion evident on his face. "What do you mean?"

Well, in for a penny, as they said. Taking a deep breath, Maddy rushed into it, prepared to lay out her well-thought-out reasons for her outrageous suggestion. "This is probably going to sound strange and demanding, but the truth is, I'd like to hire you, full-time. I know you're a professional, and you're *very* good at what you do." *Oh, so very good.* "And judging by the number of women fighting over you at the auction, you probably stay just as busy as you want and never lack for…clients."

His eyes widened. That was all. So she hurried on, logically explaining her needs, her inhibitions, her conditions, her desires. She spoke quickly, not looking at him, keeping her attention somewhere over his right shoulder, at the horizon, her voice almost tripping over itself as she rushed to get it all out before she lost her nerve.

"So you see," she said, finally reaching the conclusion of what she hoped was a persuasive, reasonable speech. "It really makes sense for both of us. You'll make your usual fee—whatever that is, I'm sure I can afford it. And I'll have a companion without any messy, silly feelings or jealousies coming into play. We'll enjoy each other for a month and walk away satisfied."

Or…maybe not. Maybe neither one of them would want to walk away. Maybe they'd actually decide they liked one another enough to continue seeing one another—sleeping together—without her having to *buy* more time. And with him *choosing* not to see anyone else.

Not falling in love, never that, but at least falling into a relationship built on mutual attraction and genuine desire. Rather than mutual attraction and genuine greed.

But she didn't say that, not wanting to scare the man off before he'd even had a chance to consider her offer.

He was obviously thinking about it now. Thinking carefully. Jake's brown eyes were narrowed in concentration, his mouth grimly set, his jaw tight, but not flexing with anger. That was something at least. He merely appeared intense, as if looking at this situation from every angle, the way she had.

"Let me make sure I understand," he said, his voice gravelly and thick. "You would like to pay me a large sum of money to have sex with you for the next thirty days."

"With *only* me," she clarified.

"Right. Sex with *only* you. A *lot* of sex. All *kinds* of crazy sex."

She couldn't be blushing. She hadn't blushed since she was a twelve-year-old whose budding figure had attracted the very verbal notice of the boys in her class. It was merely the heat of the summer day hitting her cheeks. God, *please* let her not be blushing, not now that she'd come this far.

"Well, not just sex." *But mostly sex.* She thought quickly, scrambling for other duties he could fulfill, to make the whole thing worth his while and to convince him that she wasn't just asking out of the selfish, helpless want that had filled her from the moment they'd met.

She lit upon the perfect thing. "My sister's wedding! It's in two weeks, and I desperately need an escort. You can be my date. That's within your purview, isn't it?"

He tsked-tsked lightly. "Buying another date with me, hmm?"

"Well, you are a paid escort, right? Isn't that your usual job title? You'd actually be *escorting* me, rather than, well, you know, just…"

"Screwing you."

That was very crude. It was also very exciting, almost dangerous. She'd never had a man treat her with anything but gentlemanly restraint, but she sensed that, if she wanted to let him, Jake could be much more aggressive—*wildly* so.

"But I suppose I could live with being arm candy for a society wedding."

He'd be a perfect escort, tall and strong and utterly magnificent in a tux, she knew.

She would *not* think about Tabby laughing her ass off over this, or about Deborah choking on her chateaubriand. There was too much at stake right now. Even more than Maddy had suspected, given the way she could barely breathe.

"So, what do you say? You'd be doing me an enormous favor," she insisted, hoping she wasn't babbling. "You already know as well as I do that I have no use for the typical games—romance and love and such. I'm a businesswoman and this is a business proposal I'm making."

"Strictly business. That's the only way you want it."

Gulping, she nodded. It wasn't exactly a lie.

If she and Jake decided at the end of their thirty days that there was more to this than lust, maybe she'd find her way clear to at least consider dipping her toes in romance waters again. Maybe.

Really, when she thought about it, this was the perfect way to build up to that—with no risk. No embarrassment. No scenes or breakups. It was like getting to test-drive a sporty little Mercedes for a month without getting her heart set on the pretty pink color. Without expecting it to possibly look as good to her in thirty days as it did the day she'd first set eyes on it.

And without letting anybody else behind the wheel until she'd figured out if she could afford it.

"So, constant wild sex and a date to a wedding for…how much?"

Constant wild sex…*think, damn it*. She quickly named a figure off the top of her head, figuring he had to make at *least* what a top executive at the bank would make. But she suddenly remembered that before she had stepped into the fray at the auction, the bid had been over five thousand dollars for one *date* with the man. Thinking of that, and how incredibly he'd made love to her, she worried she'd offered far too little.

He didn't respond by so much as the quirk of a muscle.

"If that's not enough…"

"It's enough," he snapped. "Let me ask you something, Maddy. Why do you think…" He cleared his throat, started again. "How is it that you *know* so much about me? I mean, about who I am and what I *do*?"

"My sister told me."

"Gotta love that sister of yours. How'd *she* know?"

"One of the auction sponsors told her about the infamous male escort, and Tabby found out in advance what number you'd be. And, of course, the bio in the program fit." Smiling ruefully, she added, "I'm afraid it wouldn't take much for the rich women of this town to ferret you out."

"The bio," he murmured, rubbing his hand against his jaw. "What did it say again?"

"I don't remember exactly. Just something about you being a world traveler, someone who appreciates fine wine and beautiful women. It also claimed that you were European. But I've decided that must just be part of your character—the role you play. Because if you're anything but a beer-drinking all-American boy, I'm Mary Poppins."

"Busted, Mary," he muttered, "I guess you're too smart for me." He crossed his arms over his big chest, still leaving her hanging, not responding to her offer. She wondered if he liked to torture bunnies in his spare time, too.

"One more question. If you were set on buying my *services*, why did you run out on me the night of the auction without even telling me your name? Did you get cold feet?" He sounded almost hopeful, for some reason, as if this answer was more important than anything else. "Did you have a change of heart about doing something so…reckless?"

She shook her head, not sure how much to admit. Especially since he might be meeting her family members—her father and his wife—at Tabitha's wedding.

That, however, was the real problem. She couldn't let him walk into such a situation unprepared and unaware. "I wasn't buying you for myself."

He closed his eyes slowly, his lips moving as he mumbled under his breath.

"What was that?"

"I was counting to ten."

"Why?"

"Never mind." His tone weary, he asked, "Who were you *buying* me for?"

Maddy twisted her hands, leaning against the back of the captain's chair and gazed around. Her father used to love this boat—but his new wife didn't like to sail. And Deborah had made it clear that she also didn't like her husband going out on the water in a vessel named for another woman, even one who had died years and years ago.

"Let me guess. It was your sister's idea."

"How did you know that?"

"Intuition. So how come she didn't do it herself?"

"She didn't want to cheat on her fiancé."

The eyes closed again. The mouth moved. She'd swear she could make out the words *eleven* and *twelve* before he looked at her once more. "How noble of her."

She was going about this all wrong, nervousness making her skip around the point instead of getting right to it. So she bit the bullet. She told him—just enough to make him understand how important this was, important enough to make her take chances she'd never have chosen to take.

When she'd finished telling him about her father, his new wife, as well as Bitsy Wellington and her crowd, she concluded, "So there was no intention by either me, or by Tabby, to do anything other than make sure your services were not engaged by our father's wife." A bit grudgingly, she added, "Only Tabby didn't trust herself not to remain entirely *selfless* about the whole thing. And I did."

Jake didn't close his eyes this time. He didn't mumble, he didn't count. And he stopped doing that clenching thing with his jaw. The broad shoulders relaxed just a bit, and, if she looked hard, she thought she might see the edges of his mouth twitch up in the tiniest smile.

"I see. And everything that happened afterward—you and me—was because you couldn't trust yourself after all?"

Ah. Now she knew why he was looking so relaxed. Because he'd figured her out. He'd seen through all the rest and come to the most important point.

"Yes." She lifted a hand and placed it on his chest, right above his strongly beating heart. "Everything we shared afterward happened because I was attracted to you. I *wanted* you. And I still do."

He moved closer, until their bodies brushed lightly, the warm summer air only an inch wide between them. Laughing softly, he reached up and stroked her hair. "Oh, Maddy, you crazy woman. How can you be so smart and yet so totally *nuts?*"

She remained stiff, not melting into him as her instincts were telling her to. Was he saying yes? Or no?

"I'm not taking your money."

"Oh, yes, you are. You must. I absolutely insist, or it's no deal."

His hand hovered in the air, close to her hair, no longer touching her. "You don't mean that."

"Yes, I do. I brought my checkbook and I intend to pay you up front the minute you agree."

"You're telling me that if I don't say yes, you won't ever see me again? You'll buy me…but you won't date me? Do you have any idea how insane that sounds?"

She did. It *was* insane and so far out of character for her, she hardly even recognized herself.

But that didn't change her mind. Maddy needed to set the boundaries, the protective ground rules that would let her get out of this in thirty days with her heart and her pride intact if things didn't work out. As, she already suspected given her history, they would not.

"It's this way or no way, Jake," she said, her tone firm, her back ramrod stiff. He was now talking to the tough negotiator. The ice queen.

She kind of ruined the moment by adding, "I'm not looking for a…a boyfriend."

He gave her a gesturing look.

"Or even a real lover."

"We're lovers, babe."

"Business associates with benefits."

He threw his head back and laughed, which made the thick muscles in his neck quiver and brought Maddy's attention to the beads of sweat gathering in the hollow of his throat. Oh, how she wanted to sample it. And then sample everything else.

But she still didn't have his answer.

"Well?"

"I couldn't be at your beck and call 24-7," he warned. "I have other obligations. Quite a full schedule." Obviously seeing her frown, he clarified. "Of course, if we were to come to an agreement, I'd guarantee that none of those other *obligations* would ever involve sexual contact with anyone else. Otherwise, a lot of my time has to be my own. And that *is* a deal-breaker."

Of course he had a private life, everyone did. She already knew he had a family, *somewhere*. And maybe he really did have other clients that he "escorted" without any of the naughty goings-on. She could live with that…she hoped.

"Very well."

"Also, just so we're clear, *if* I agree to this *solution* of yours, you won't be calling all the shots." He raked a hot stare across her, from her windblown hair, down to the clingy top, which outlined the red bikini beneath. "You might be paying for my un-divided attention when we're together. But how I choose to *pay* that attention is up to me."

Maddy shivered lightly, despite the warmth of the day. The words might have been cool, but the look in his eyes was hot. *So* hot. And she knew he was telling her he'd be the one in charge in the bedroom.

Well. She'd bow to the expert on that. She'd be insane not to, especially after the amazing things he'd done to her Tuesday night. "Also agreed," she managed to whisper, already feeling weak in the knees at the thought of him *paying atten-tion* to her.

"One last point."

"Yes?"

"If I'm not seeing anyone else, you're not either."

That surprised her, considering she hadn't had so much as a date in more than a year, not until Jake. It also surprised her that he'd care. She wondered if he had started feeling the crazy mix of emotions toward her that she already felt for him. The question also definitely reiterated that he would not be merely an *employee*.

Maddy nodded slowly. "Okay. Does that mean…"

"Yeah, I guess it does." He reached for her again, sliding his fingers into her hair, cupping her head, then dragging her forward until her body was crushed against his. "You've got a deal, Madeline Turner," he whispered.

Then he covered her mouth with his…and sealed that deal with an earth-shattering kiss.

A GOOD MAN WOULD HAVE TOLD Maddy the truth right away. A noble man would have stopped her before she'd ever made her offer. A kind man would have taken pity and not tormented her with questions and conditions while she awaited his answer. And a gentleman would have absolutely refused.

Jake considered himself good. At least a little noble. Pretty kind, especially to the injured and helpless. And definitely a gentleman, given his upbringing.

But he'd kept his big mouth shut. He had, in fact, forced himself not to laugh as Ms. Madeline Turner "bought" him for the next thirty days.

Oh, he hadn't been laughing at first. The idea that he'd been mistaken for a male hooker—well, that still burned. If it hadn't resulted in him ending up with this amazing—strong-yet-vulnerable, demure-yet-sexy, icy-and-blazing-hot-woman—he'd probably be pretty damned furious. As it was, he definitely had something to say to the auction people, who'd apparently gotten his information mixed up with that of some Euro-trash gigolo. Possibly even the Irish-sounding guy who'd gone on the block immediately after him.

Hmm…he wondered what that dude—billed as the Chicago firefighter offering beer and baseball—had gone for. And how Mr. Smooth had felt about it.

At that, he really did laugh.

"Beautiful, isn't it?" Maddy asked, obviously hearing him as they skimmed across the surface of the clear, calm water. The sun beat down from above, yet with the speed of the wind in the sails, and the rush of air moving past, he didn't feel the heat.

Well, unless he looked at *her*.

Maddy had taken off her shirt and wore just a pair of soft white shorts and a flaming red bikini top that couldn't possibly manage to hold in all her curves at once. Good thing she hadn't done it while they were docked. There probably would have been a yacht traffic jam caused by all the sailors ogling her as they sailed out of the marina.

He'd thanked the universe more than once today, even if he wasn't entirely sure what the hell the universe was up to, given the crazy situation in which he'd suddenly found himself.

"You really love this, don't you?" he asked, watching her turn her face into the wind and let it blow her hair in a long, billowing stream of lush brown behind her.

Here on the water, she seemed fully in her element, completely caught up in what she was doing. Obviously the woman knew her way around this vessel and she had unerringly led them far from shore. She'd given him orders, and he'd followed, not sure which was sexier—her amazing body, or the way she barked commands, so sure she was in charge.

Maybe of the boat. Nothing else.

"I do. How about you? Feeling all right?" she asked. "I know some people get a little seasick."

"I'm fine." Jake wasn't stupid—he'd grabbed some motion sickness pills on the way to the marina.

"Good."

Eyes on the horizon, Maddy absently lifted her hands and caught her hair between them, twisting it and tucking it into a loose bun at her nape. Every move was smooth and fluid, as elegant and graceful as the *Magdalena* herself.

Jake couldn't help it. He reached out and ran his fingers through the silky strand veil, pulling it back down.

"Hey!"

"I like seeing the wind blow through your hair," he explained simply.

She licked her lips, but didn't protest. "Oh."

The hair stayed down.

They continued traveling for another hour, not really talking, not really needing to. Jake suspected they were both still replaying the conversation they'd had back on shore. What they'd agreed to. What it had meant and where it would lead. Not just in thirty days…but now.

She'd hired him. But that had nothing to do with the fantasies playing in his mind. Fantasies about laying her down on a thick towel, plucking the strings of her bikini and revealing her magnificent body to the wide-open sky. And his hungry gaze.

Being in bed with her the other night had been fantastic. Plunging into her beneath the brilliant sun, feeling the heat on his back that couldn't rival the heat in her tight channel, would be absolutely mind-blowing.

Though he couldn't exactly see, because of her dark sunglasses, he felt sure Maddy was watching him. She stole several long glances at him, especially when he pulled his own shirt off and let the sun warm his bare skin.

With her stare affecting him as powerfully as a touch, he suspected her visions—fantasies—mirrored his.

He didn't say a thing, didn't suggest they stop, didn't tell her how much he wanted her. Instead he let them both think on it awhile. Build it. Anticipate it.

They'd be dying for it when the time came.

And that time seemed to be now. Maddy wordlessly adjusted the sails to slow their speed. "Are you hungry?" she asked, not even looking in his direction. "I brought some lunch. We could stop for a while to eat."

Stop for a while. 'Bout damn time. "Put it on autopilot and busy ourselves some other way, you mean?"

Her laugh was thin. Weak and breathy. "Uh…something like that." She nodded toward the cabin. "There's a bag on the counter, and another in the fridge. Would you mind getting them?"

Jake did as she asked, awed once again that the cabin of this boat was bigger than the living room in his small apartment. And more richly furnished. There was a large, comfortable-looking bed, but it didn't tempt him. Not yet. He wanted to have Maddy on the hard planking of the deck, the only ceiling above them a vivid blue one streaked with golden sunshine.

"Got it?" she called from above.

"Coming." He glanced into the bag on the counter, spying fresh bread, fancy crackers…and a box of condoms. "Oh, I'm definitely coming."

Retrieving a bag of cheese and fruit from the fridge, plus an icy bottle of champagne and two glasses, he brought everything up on deck. When he spied the name on the label and the pricy brand of cheese, he whistled. "You do sail prepared." Putting the food down on a small table between two lounge chairs, he murmured, "You must have been pretty sure I'd say yes to your proposal."

"Actually," she admitted, "I had originally planned to whisk you out here onto the water and ply you with food and alcohol before I asked you."

Her amusing, matter-of-fact tone took the sting out of her surprisingly honest confession. "If you'd taken off those shorts, it probably would have worked."

Laughing softly, Maddy reached for the button at her waist and unfastened it. A quick flick of her fingers and the cotton fabric fell to puddle at her feet, and was then kicked away.

"Oh, God," he whispered, pushing his sunglasses onto the top of his head with his index finger. Then he could only stare in voracious hunger at the curve of her hips, the line of her thighs, the hollow above her groin where the fabric of her bikini ended. Not at all stick-thin, she was just so damned womanly, curvy and soft, made to cushion a man in welcome.

The woman simply took his breath away.

"It *definitely* would have worked," he finally muttered.

Maddy reached into the bag, grabbed a grape and popped it

into her mouth. Sighing in pleasure at the cool sweetness, she took another one, licking the juice that squirted from it off her lips, then sat in one of the lounge chairs. She stretched out like a cat in a pool of warm sunshine. "I know. But I couldn't go through with it."

He couldn't take his eyes off her long enough to ask why.

She explained anyway. "I wanted you to really think about my idea, not be seduced into accepting it." She offered him an impish smile. "If you'd said no, however, I might just have shanghaied you and tried to change your mind."

"If I had said no, I'd have deserved to be struck dead on the spot." Jake sat on the end of her chair, ignoring his own. "You really thought I'd refuse?"

"You almost did. Didn't you."

Yeah. He almost had. At least until the whole story had come out and he'd begun to understand *why* Maddy had been treating him like a gigolo. Then he'd been amused and ready to tell her the truth—that he was a simple paramedic and that being with her for the next thirty days, or thirty years, he'd begun to suspect, would be entirely his pleasure.

Her bald refusal to even consider letting him close without paying him, however, had quickly squelched that idea. He didn't entirely understand her reasoning, but he had at least a suspicion about what was driving her.

Maddy's self-protective walls had been built brick by brick with the help of her father and her hard-edged sister, not to mention all the jaded people she'd been surrounded with all her life. Then there was whatever secret hurt she'd suffered in a past relationship—he knew there was one. She hadn't opened up about it yet, but he didn't doubt she'd been burned. Badly.

So she was protecting herself. In the only way she knew how. She was hiding behind the wall built of her money and her icy reputation, keeping him on the other side. Not about to genuinely trust anyone enough to try a real relationship—especially not someone she thought was a damned male whore.

If she set the boundaries, went in expecting no emotion, no true feelings, she couldn't be hurt.

God, his heart ached for her. He wanted to take her into his arms and hold her, assure her that not every man was like the ones she'd known before. Let her know she could trust him— that he was *not* who she thought he was, not by a long shot.

Part of him suspected she'd be relieved, happy, willing to accept that he was an average guy who was falling for her. Another part of him feared she'd shove him off the boat…and out of her life for good.

Jake wasn't about to take that chance. And *that* was why he'd gone along with the insanity.

"I didn't. And I'm here," he finally said, thrusting away the momentary guilt about not opening up to her. He would…soon. Just as soon as he'd convinced her to give him a shot—a real one—and made sure she knew he would never intentionally hurt her. As *someone* obviously had.

"I'm glad."

She pulled her sunglasses off as she leaned toward him. Jake met her halfway, brushing his mouth across hers, tasting a bit of the grape juice on her lips. Deepening the kiss, he tasted a bit more, swirling his tongue against hers, falling right back into that deep well of warm, sensual pleasure he'd been missing since Wednesday morning.

Maddy shifted a little in the lounge chair, but he didn't realize she'd reached around to untie her bikini top until it fell into her lap. He sat back, watching the sun warm her breasts. She appeared almost pagan, despite the fragile paleness of her skin. "You're doing more than waving hello to the sun out your window today."

"Yes, I am." She smiled, obviously also remembering their conversation in her office.

He reached for the bottle of sunscreen they'd both applied earlier. "You'd better let me help you put more lotion on. I couldn't even imagine you getting sunburned here."

"Thank you *so* much for thinking about my well-being," she replied sweetly, a hint of wickedness in her eyes.

Jake squeezed a small handful of the milky white fluid into one palm, then rubbed both hands together to spread it between them. Inhaling the tropical scents of citrus and coconut, he reached out and touched her breast, smoothing the protective coating over her sensitive skin. Maddy's head dropped back, her mouth opening on a deep, sensual sigh. "Mmm."

Her nipples grew taut as he lotioned her, and he allowed himself a few pleasurable strokes, tweaking the puckered skin that demanded his attention. "Jake," she whimpered, "please, more."

"I'm not quite finished." He kept on stroking lightly, not giving her the more urgent caress he knew she was dying for. The woman really needed to learn patience.

Reaching again for the bottle, he started over again on her other breast. But this time, once he was sure he'd protected every luscious inch, he bent low, close enough to scrape his tongue across the rock-hard tip.

She jerked. "Yes!"

Still cupping her, caressing her, loving the complete absence of friction the lotion provided, Jake gently sucked her into his mouth. Soft at first, he increased the tension when she arched up against him, demanding it.

"Oh, please," she groaned, twining her hands in his hair as he went back and forth, kissing, laving, suckling her hard enough to draw a series of shocked gasps from her mouth.

Knowing the arms of the chaise lounge would soon get in the way, Jake let Maddy go long enough to toss a large, colorful beach towel down onto the deck. Jake rose to his feet, reached for her hand and tugged her up, too.

Rather than leading her to the towel right away, however, he began kissing his way down her body, much as he had the other night, until he was on his knees in front of her. This time, however, when he reached the fabric of her string bikini, he did not veer away. Catching the elastic in his fingers, he pushed it down, nibbling his way all the way down to the juncture of her thighs, rubbing his lips against the soft thatch between them.

Her hands fell to his shoulders. She made no effort to pull away. They'd come much too far for those kinds of inhibitions. "Taste me, please," she said.

Taste her? He intended to devour her.

He was smiling in pure hunger as he spied the glistening pearl of flesh half-concealed by her soft curls. Still smiling, he dipped close, flicked his tongue out. Her nails clenched into his muscles and she groaned.

Reaching for her calf, Jake gently encircled it with his hand, lifting her foot onto the seat of the lounge she'd just vacated. Opening her for his most intimate dining pleasure.

Maddy groaned, the sound low and desperate. "I think the ground would be shaking even if we were on dry land."

Holding her by the hips to keep her steady, Jake tilted her closer, right where he wanted her, and explored her pretty, slick folds with his mouth. As he'd expected, she nearly buckled at the sensation, but he kept her steady, completely in control. And he didn't relent, just kept pleasuring her until he heard her cry out her climax a few moments later.

"Beautiful," he murmured against her thigh, watching as she shook from the power of it.

He let go of her hips, pulled her down and onto her back on the deck. She stretched again, easing this way and that, her body warm and pliant and, he would suspect, still pulsing from her powerful orgasm.

Usually he liked to go very, very, slow, but right now, Jake wanted to share the moment, to be part of her deep pleasure. So he pushed his trunks down, not even kicking them all the way off. Using his teeth to tear open one of the condoms he'd brought up from the galley, he sheathed himself and moved between Maddy's legs. Her eyes remained closed, her mouth open, her entire body flush with satisfaction.

And Jake joined right in. Pushing into her. Watching the way her hungry smile widened, and her brown eyes opened to stare up at him as his cock filled her, stretched her, mated with her.

He drove home. Hard. She thrust up to meet him. Hard.

As he'd expected, the afternoon sun sent blazing heat into his back, but it couldn't compare to the heat of Maddy's steamy, clenched core. She squeezed him from within, holding on so tightly he felt wrapped in a fist of the softest, smoothest velvet.

A cooling breeze washed over them, providing relief. Soft waves lapped against the side of the boat, making it rock beneath them. Gently. Up and down. Setting a natural rhythm to which they both began a slow, sultry dance.

Maddy's breaths grew choppy, her cheeks flushed with color. Between deep, lazy thrusts, she said, "You know, I really do like the way you pay attention."

He didn't follow at first, then suddenly remembered the terms of their deal. His demand that he be the one to call the shots— to *pay attention* as he saw fit.

"Good. Because I am an attentive guy.

Wanting to see her beautiful face above him, her brown hair haloed by sunshine, he wrapped an arm around her and scooped her against him. He rolled onto his back, settling her onto his groin without ever losing their deep connection.

"Mmm," she said, lifting her hands to her hair, scooping it back, holding it off her neck to cool her skin. *Beautiful.*

She remained still, sitting straight up on him and not moving, visibly savoring the new position. Jake reached for her breasts, stroking and playing with her nipples while Maddy began to ride him. With restraint he didn't know she possessed, she pulled up until he almost slid out of her entirely. He actually felt the cool breeze blowing on his wet cock, before she slid back down to wrap him in her warmth once again.

"You've learned the value of slowing down," he murmured, unable to prevent a smile as he watched her.

Maddy nodded. "Mmm, hmm. I'm a fast learner."

"I'm glad to hear it."

Maybe she'd be open to learning a few more things from him. Things that had nothing to do with moments like this—moments of pure sensual bliss. Perhaps she'd someday allow him to teach her a little more about relationships, romance, the human heart. Maybe even the existence of love.

He had thirty days in which to try. And so far, Jake thought he was off to a pretty good start.

9

OVER THE NEXT SEVERAL DAYS, Maddy remembered what it was like to be a woman. A sensual—sexual—woman. Rather than a bank drone, a dutiful daughter, a supportive sister.

She and Jake had spent the entire weekend together, staying out on the boat Saturday night rather than coming in to shore. Whatever his *obligations* were, he'd at least had Saturday and Sunday free. They'd sailed and laughed, talked and made exquisite love. But on Monday, he'd disappeared again, saying he'd be busy for the next two days—another forty-eight hour commitment—and promised to see her in a few days.

She'd forced herself not to think about where he was, who he was with and what he was doing. Jake had given his word that he'd have no sexual contact with anyone else, but that didn't mean he wasn't *seeing* anyone else. Professionally. Or personally.

Lord, she hadn't even asked him if he was involved in any kind of relationship. She'd focused solely on his, um, *job*.

Let it go, she'd reminded herself many times. No way would he have agreed to the terms if he was seriously involved with another woman. Besides, there was nothing she could do, anyway. She simply had to trust him.

Honestly, she did. The man had taken her check, which had both relieved and broken her heart a little. Mainly, though, it had been a relief, because it had sealed their bargain. While trusting any man was not easy for her, especially after Oliver, Maddy *did* have confidence in her business judgment.

He'd stick to his end of the deal. She knew it.

And *that's* how she managed to get through the forty-eight hours without driving herself crazy wondering if he was on the arm of some rich old hag like Bitsy Wellington, explaining that he couldn't provide any more *intimate* services.

Fortunately, all those worries had disappeared on Wednesday night. He'd shown up at her door with a new-release DVD, a big bag filled with popcorn, Lemonheads, Gummi Bears and other movie-theater type candy, and informed her they were having a movie date.

Since she'd answered the door in nothing but an emerald-green teddy, however, he'd decided the date could wait.

They'd made love right on the living room floor and they'd been wild, rolling helplessly across the carpet, absolutely ravenous for one another. Maddy had, as usual, been surprised by both his patience and his stamina, not sure where the man got his strength. Eventually they'd ended up right in front of the windows overlooking the twinkling lights of the city.

He'd taken her from behind, the two of them kneeling in front of all that glass and all those stars, an enormous orange moon hanging like a paper cutout right above them.

Talk about wanting to howl at the night like a wild, untamed creature. When she saw the handprints all over the windows the next day, she'd decided untamed had been a very good description.

There'd been two full nights of laughter and whispered conversation and sexual bliss, then another two nights of secretive silence. Until now. It was Sunday again, and she was driving to meet him at a local restaurant.

He'd offered to come over. But they'd both known from the other night that if she allowed that, they wouldn't eat anything until morning. Well, except each other, that is. And frankly, while that thought was incredibly appealing, she was starving for real food and her kitchen was, as usual, pretty empty.

Besides, they had all night. For now, she just wanted to enjoy his company, in public, as if they were any other couple.

You're not.

"Yeah, yeah," she muttered to the skeptical voice in her head as she entered the restaurant promptly at seven o'clock, her gaze traveling the crowded establishment in search of his familiar broad shoulders and short, thick hair.

"What?"

She hadn't even realized he'd been standing in the vestibule until he'd stepped beside her and touched her arm.

"Hi."

"Hi yourself." Despite the crowd, he bent and brushed a gentle kiss across her lips. When it ended, instead of pulling away, he brushed his nose against hers in a sweet, tender gesture—an Eskimo kiss, she remembered from her childhood, having dim memories of sharing them with her mother. She melted a little on the spot.

"Shall we get a table?"

"Absolutely! I'm famished."

"That mean you're not having a salad?"

Maddy elbowed him in the ribs as they approached the hostess station to request a table. Before they reached it, however, Jake's cell phone rang. "I'll turn it off," he muttered, "I'm not on call tonight…."

Maddy put her hand up to stop him from saying anything further. She did not want to know about his "on call" time. "It's okay."

"Uh-oh," he said, reading the number. "I probably should take this."

Maddy smiled at the hostess, requesting a table for two while Jake stepped to the corner to take the call. Trying not to listen, she couldn't help overhearing a few snippets of the conversation. Words like "sweetie" and "honey, it'll be okay, you know I'm here for you," making her ears perk up as if she were James Bond's partner in spying.

The words were bad enough. The soft, gentle tone, however, truly bothered her. She did not like to think of him using *that* voice with any other woman. And she had no doubt it *was* another woman he was talking to.

"You know, why don't you give that table to someone else?" she told the hostess, her back stiffening. She'd lost her appetite.

"That's a good idea," Jake said, snapping his phone closed and giving her a grateful look as he returned to her side.

Huh. She wondered how grateful he'd be if she took the phone from his fingers and pitched it into the restaurant's tropical fish tank.

"We've got to go."

"We?" Her brow arching, she added, "Are you sure you don't need to go alone? I'm quite capable of seeing myself home—I have my own car."

He shook his head, taking her arm to lead her outside. "No, I'm not letting you get away, I've been looking forward to this date since I left your place Friday morning." He opened the door for her, waited while she exited, and followed her out into the night. "It shouldn't take long." Frowning, he added, "I hope."

"Look, Jake, I know this is just business and everything, but if you have to go deal with one of your other…clients…I'd really prefer not to go along for the ride. I'm not the type of woman who'll wait in the car while you dash inside and explain to Mrs. Robinson that you can't be at her beck and call tonight."

He froze, his jaw dropping open. Which was when she realized she'd made a big mistake. "I thought…I mean…"

"You honestly thought I was going to take you along while I went to meet a *client*."

"You were so *tender* on the phone, I assumed…"

"It was my baby sister, Jenny. She just had a big fight with her boyfriend. He drove away and stranded her down at the Navy Pier. She was bawling her eyes out and asked me to come get her and take her back to her dorm."

Jake shook his head, disappointment so clear in his expression she could almost feel it washing over her. "I'm *so* sorry. I can be such a bitch." She swallowed and stepped toward her own car. "Why don't I go home and you can call me later…if you want to."

Grabbing her arm, Jake stopped her, stepping in close and cupping her face in his hand. He pressed a quick, hard kiss on her lips. "Shut up. Just drive me there. My truck's not big enough, and you, at least, have that little backseat. We'll take care of Jenny, then go back to your place." His eyes narrowed and he kissed her again, licking roughly at her tongue, then muttering against her lips, "And I'll pay you back for your lack of faith in me."

So relieved that she hadn't ruined their evening completely, she smiled tremulously. They got in the car, Maddy behind the wheel, as she started the engine and backed out of the parking lot. Before they'd even reached the street, her good mood had returned. "How are you going to pay me back?"

"I'm going to torture you," he replied, his tone bored, his attention out the window.

"Torture?"

He finally looked over, his eyes shimmering in the light thrown off the car's dashboard. "I know it drives you crazy when I go slow. Well, tonight, I'm going so slow you'll think I'm moving backward."

Her thighs quivered. "Monster."

"Yeah. That's me." He dropped a hand on her thigh. "Drive quick, okay? She sounded pretty upset."

"You said this is the youngest one? How old is she?"

"Twenty. There's an eight-year gap between her and me. My older sisters and I call her the accident."

Hmm…that made him twenty-eight. Just her age.

"Funny that she called you, rather than one of your sisters," she mused. Whenever Tabitha had a breakup, she always showed up at Maddy's place with a bottle of tequila and a thousand dollars' worth of cosmetics from Sephora, for the "girl's night" she needed to get over it.

"She's embarrassed. My sisters can't stand the guy she's been dating and they'll say 'I told you so.' And my parents would hold it against him, if and when they do get back together. Which, knowing Jenny, will probably be soon."

Her father was exactly the same way. The one time they'd run into Oliver after he'd done Maddy so wrong, her dad had called him a scum-sucking, lowlife, bootlicking coward. For starters.

Maddy had stopped his tirade. Eventually.

"But you like the guy?"

"Hell, no. He's a lazy punk and I can't stand him."

"Then why did she call you?"

"Because *she* doesn't know I can't stand him. I know how to keep my mouth shut and mind my own business."

"Unlike your sisters—women—is that what you mean?" she asked, not really offended but enjoying putting him on the spot.

Not that he ever stayed there for long.

"Your words. Not mine. Speaking of which—I don't have to ask you to keep the details of our, uh, arrangement, private, do I? My family doesn't know about…"

"Enough said." She wasn't bothered by the question. Of course, he had to be sure. Besides, he didn't sound as though he was truly worried she'd out him as a hooker to his kid sister. "I'm just your dinner date." The words provided her a good opening to do a little sneaky prying, and she wasn't about to let it go. "They won't think it's strange, uh, you being with me? I mean, you don't have anyone they usually see you with?"

He saw right through her. As usual. Laughing softly and

tucking her hair behind one ear, he murmured, "I haven't been involved with anyone for a long time."

Why it so relieved her that he hadn't had a girlfriend, she didn't want to think about.

"And Maddy? You're more than just my dinner date," he whispered. "Much more."

Keeping her eyes on the road, Maddy couldn't help smiling a tiny bit, if only on the inside.

Because Jake was already ever-so-much-more to her, too.

"WHY ARE GUYS such assholes?"

"Like I've always said, babe. A.M.A.S.," Jake replied. "All Men Are Scum."

"You're not!" Jenny scooted up from the tiny backseat, her elbows on her knees as she leaned between him and Maddy. "He's not, right?"

"Definitely not," Maddy replied, entering the conversation for the first time.

Not that she could have gotten a word in before now. They'd picked up Jenny ten minutes ago. From the moment she'd gotten into the car, she'd been crying and blowing her nose into a Taco Bell napkin she dug out of her purse. Then babbling and raging, explaining the fight—something about a girl named Liz and a party and a kiss—and generally acting like the high-strung twenty-year-old she was.

Maddy had remained quiet, driving, making occasional commiserating noises and frowning in sympathy with the slightly hysterical young woman she'd never laid eyes on before. She was calm and reasonable, totally in control, as always, but warm, too.

Well, almost always in control. He'd definitely made her lose it on a few occasions. And he could hardly wait to do so again.

"Who are you, anyway?" Jenny asked, finally distracted from her tale of woe. "Is this your car? It's wicked sweet. Jake, is she your girlfriend? How long have you been together?" She sighed deeply, the melodrama oozing out. "Oh, God, I interrupted your date, didn't I? Why is he *such* an asshole?"

She threw herself back into her seat.

"This is Madeline Turner…I introduced you when you got in, remember?" Jake asked, unable to hide his amusement.

Jenny just sniffed. "Sorry. Wasn't listening."

"No kidding."

"It's all right," Maddy said. "I'm glad to meet you, but I'm very sorry it's under these circumstances."

"Men suck."

"They certainly do." Maddy cast him a quick, apologetic glance and clarified. "Some of them."

"Not Jake, I know," said his baby sister. "He's a doll. I think it's having sisters. In my opinion, every woman should end up with a man who had sisters. They drain all the assholeness out of him while he's growing up and make him learn to treat a woman right."

Maddy chuckled. "There's no denying your brother is a perfect gentleman." Pursing her lips, she added, "And you know, come to think of it, *my* ex was an only child."

"You see?" Jenny exclaimed, throwing her hands up in the air. "So is Toby."

Toby being he of the great assholeness.

But Jake was more interested in hearing about Maddy's ex. This was the first time she'd mentioned him, though he'd strongly suspected the guy's actions left some major damage.

Had he been a lover? Fiancé? He couldn't even contemplate the idea that someone else might have actually put a wedding ring on her beautiful finger and then let her get away.

Jenny was fine, already showing more interest in the car than in the boyfriend who would be texting her and asking for forgiveness within a few hours, he was quite sure. He wanted to know more about Maddy. "So, tell me more about this ex."

"Oh-ho, haven't gotten that far in the relationship, huh? Just sex talk, no ex-talk?"

"It's been a long time since I've threatened your life," Jake said, not even turning around to glare at his sister. His words were menacing enough. "Now be quiet or I'll call Heather and Blair and sic them on you tonight."

Jenny stiffened, definitely fearing the combined threat of their two older sisters, complete busybodies, both of them. "Sorry. Go ahead, Maddy."

"Go ahead with what?" she asked, obviously distracted by the sibling bickering. With only one sister—and a snooty, pretentious, pushy one at that, judging by what he'd heard about her— Jake doubted Maddy had much experience with the playfully cutthroat world of sibling disputes.

"The ex. What was he, a cheat?" Jenny asked.

Jake didn't scold her, because that was exactly the question he wanted to ask, but hadn't dared to.

Maddy sighed softly. "Oh, yes. Oliver was most definitely a cheat."

Jenny gasped. "Oh, God, did he cheat on you with a *dude?*"

That startled a shocked laugh out of their driver. "No, why on earth would you ask that?"

"Well, come on, I mean, *Oliver?* Only a parent who's just *begging* for a gay son would come up with that name!"

Jake snorted, quickly hiding his laughter when Maddy swept a sidelong glance his way. Her tiny frown told him she'd seen his amusement.

"Well, as far as I know, he confined his cheating to snow bunnies and cocktail waitresses."

"But you're so hot. Why would any guy do that?"

Maddy shifted in her seat, as always, not accepting that she was a beautiful, desirable woman. "He liked tall, rail-thin, leggy blondes."

"Then it sounds to me like he should have been with an albino greyhound," Jake snapped, completely despising the unknown Oliver. "Because he's only fit to be with his own kind…dogs."

"I totally agree. You are so much better than that," Jenny said, whether out of loyalty to Maddy because she was with Jake, or because she liked her—or her car—or simply out of a go-girl-all-men-suck attitude.

Maybe all of the above.

"I think it was a combination of immaturity, selfishness and greed," Maddy admitted, her voice low, almost as if she was speaking to herself. "I am sure he liked my connections and my family money more than me."

"She's rich?" Jenny piped in.

"Shut up, Jen."

His sister shut up.

"But he was a spoiled rich kid who took what he wanted when he wanted it. While he very briefly thought he wanted me, he obviously changed his mind and moved on…without clueing me in."

"How'd you find out?"

Jake hadn't asked, Jenny had. Again he did not tell her to shut up, because he wanted to know the answer. He couldn't possibly have asked—he was too busy keeping his jaw clamped shut and his body tightly pressed against the passenger seat, so damned furious at the lousy prick who'd hurt Maddy he couldn't even speak.

Maddy glanced into the rearview mirror, seeming to meet his sister's eyes. "He went on a ski trip and I decided to 'surprise' him by coming up to join him. He was surprised all right."

"Eww! Did you walk in when they were…"

"Jenny," Jake snapped, "that's a little too personal."

"Sorry. Man, I'm ready to run out of hope altogether. If it can happen to you, it can totally happen to anyone."

The Maddy he'd met a few weeks ago—the hard, brittle

one—probably would have nodded in agreement. The cool woman he'd walked with to the park, who'd slammed the very idea of lasting love as being a fantasy might have warned his baby sister about being cautious, staying slightly separate from anyone to avoid getting hurt.

Instead, she surprised him. "You know, looking back, it was just as well. He definitely wasn't the man for me."

Ah, progress. At least she was conceding there might exist such a creature—a man for her.

"And I know it wasn't my fault and that not every man would behave that way. It was his own weakness of character."

"Well, duh!"

"So I've finally come to the point where I can let it go and forget about him." Then, grunting she added, "Which is fine, except for the fact that he is still in my social circle, and I do see him once in a while."

"Is he going to be at the wedding?" Jake asked, already relishing the prospect.

"God, I should hope not. My father would lose his mind. I think he was more furious about what Oliver did than I was. And if Dad didn't clean the floor with him, Tabitha would eviscerate him with a salad fork." Glancing again at Jenny in the mirror, she explained, "My older sister is getting married on Saturday and Jake is escorting me."

"You an escort to a rich wedding, huh?" Jenny snorted, opening her mouth to say something else.

Fearing it might be something along the lines of, "What are you going to wear, your paramedic uniform?" he quickly interrupted. "Maybe Maddy will return the favor and come with me to Blair's."

"Ugh. Don't remind me. Have you seen the bridesmaid dresses she finally decided on?" Sticking her index finger into her mouth and making retching noises, the twenty-year-old made her opinion of them clear. Then she asked Maddy, "Are you a bridesmaid?"

"Yes."

"Did your sister pick out the monkey-butt-ugliest dresses in the store? Talk about hideous—ruffled and frilly baby's-ass-peach things. They look more like something I would have worn to my third birthday party."

Soft, lyrical laughter spilled from Maddy's mouth. "No, actually the dress I'm wearing is beautiful…for someone built like Tabby."

"Meaning?"

"Meaning I'm going to have to duct tape myself to fit into it *and* to hold it up. I haven't worn a strapless, backless dress since I reached puberty."

"That sister of yours…" Jake muttered.

"Hey, it's her wedding," Maddy said with a shrug. "I honestly don't care, and it is a very pretty dress. I'll just try not to breathe. And I definitely won't be bending over. It's far too revealing for someone with my, um, figure."

Hmm…he could hardly wait to see it. What might be demure on one of those stick-thin, leggy blondes her ex had so desired would be downright sinful on a woman like Maddy. How any man could have preferred anyone else when he'd had this woman in his life, he simply had no idea.

Men who cheated pissed him off as a matter of principle. But one who'd cheated on *her?* Well, this sonofabitch Oliver was just lucky he wasn't coming to the wedding.

"I bet you'll look totally wicked," Jenny said. "While I'm going to look like Dora the Explorer in her party dress."

"Totally wicked," Jake murmured, already smiling at the thought.

"No comments, you."

In the backseat, Jenny stopped talking, and began to avidly stare down at the cell phone in her hand. The texting must have commenced. Knowing his sister was fully occupied now, Jake still kept his voice low. "I'll be happy to keep an eye on you, make sure everything stays in place."

"Mmm, hmm," Maddy said, sotto voce, watching his sister in the backseat.

"She wouldn't notice if a tidal wave came off the lake unless it filled the car and took that stupid phone out of her hands."

"Then I guess you'd better tell me where I'm going," Maddy murmured, nodding toward the sign as they entered the campus of the university Jenny attended. "Which one is her dorm?"

Jake pointed to a nearby building, and by the time they'd parked outside it, Jenny had a big grin on her face. Whatever Toby-the-asshole had said in his text messages had obviously mollified her. She'd forgiven him.

Until next week.

They got out to say goodbye to his little sister, who gave both of them enthusiastic bear hugs for coming to her rescue. Maddy, who didn't seem the type to appreciate being hugged by a complete stranger, still had a smile on her face as they got back in the car to leave.

"I like her."

"She liked you, too."

"I don't ever remember being that young and energetic."

"I disagree. You seemed like an energetic powerhouse the other night. And that day on the boat. And the night of the baseball game…"

Maddy, who hadn't seemed to be the type to even know what teasing was a few weeks ago, gave it right back to him. "Well, I fear my batteries might have run completely dry. It's going to take something pretty spectacular to charge them again."

He was up for the job. "Good. Then let's head back to your place and I'll do everything I can to…spark a charge."

"Are you saying you want to plug something in?"

Jake barked a quick laugh. "You do know you're teasing me,

right? That this is called banter. You're flirting with me and you're not talking in that snooty voice you used to use. And thank God you're not or calling me *porcine* for fantasizing about you in that bridesmaid dress."

She didn't respond at first, merely appearing to think about his words. He wondered if he should have said anything at all. The changes coming over Maddy were visible to him—maybe they hadn't been to her.

Maybe she hadn't yet acknowledged, even in her own mind, that she was opening up to him. Trusting him. Letting down her guard and being the woman he'd sensed was there, beneath the surface, all along.

From her warmth toward his sister, her men-suck commiseration, her bridesmaid talk, her openness about her bad breakup, hell, even accepting a hug without the slightest wince, Maddy was as unlike the woman he'd spoken with in her office that day as he was unlike…well, the gigolo she'd taken him for.

Maybe it's time to end this. It was definitely something to consider.

"I suppose I should thank you," she said softly. "I've been pretty cold and hard since the…incident…with Oliver." Nibbling lightly on her bottom lip, she added, "I wasn't always the ice queen."

Jake reached over and touched her cheek, lightly, briefly. "You were *never* really the ice queen."

Maddy nodded, still pensive, serious. Maybe even thinking some of the same things he'd been thinking. If she continued to think that way, she might very well be ready to hear what it was he had to tell her.

Soon. Hopefully very soon.

"You know…" he said, changing the subject to the other one that was foremost on his mind. "Thinking of you in that bridesmaid dress you were talking about has suddenly got me anxious for a preview. Let's go back to your place so you can model it for me." He made no attempt to disguise his wolfish tone or true, lustful intentions.

"What about dinner?"

Jake merely leaned back in the seat, stretching his long legs out as far as he could in the small car. "I suddenly prefer to dine in. Do you have anything…appetizing at your place?"

"Are we bantering again?"

"I think we are. Bantering, flirting, exchanging innuendo."

"Well then." She appeared to think about it, tapping the tip of her finger on her cheek. "Hmm. I believe there are still a few Lemonheads and some popcorn…"

"Or?"

"Or you *could* just dine on me."

Exactly the kind of dinner he had in mind.

"But first, we've got to clear something up, mister. You haven't cashed that check I gave you." She sounded accusing.

"You peeking in my wallet again?"

"I do manage a bank, you know."

Oh. Right.

"You'd better not even be *thinking* of trying to tear it up or hand it back to me at the end of our thirty days."

"Maddy, come on, I don't need your money."

"Tough," she snapped. "We had a deal, so you cash it. Do whatever you want with the money, invest it, pay Jenny's tuition, give it to charity for all I care. But fair's fair." Her lips curved up the tiniest bit. "I'm not a welsher."

Ah, now he understood the amusement. He'd used the exact terms when seeking her out at the bank.

"You'll do it?"

He should have expected this, he really should have. If Maddy was genuinely changing, letting her heart open up, she had to be scared to death. The first thing she'd do is try to get things back under control, protect herself, just in case. Personally, he believed they'd gone too far for her to do it—that genie was out of the bottle. She could not stop smiling at him, exchanging warm looks and sexy conversations any more than he could.

But she could remind them both of why they'd gotten into this. And that was exactly what she was doing.

"Jake?"

"Yeah, yeah," he muttered.

"You promise?"

"All right, yes, I promise," he agreed, knowing that no, he could not tell her the truth yet. Not while she still felt the need to make sure she had an easy way out at the end of their month together, just in case.

Besides, she'd certainly made no comments about them sticking together beyond that. She hadn't verbally expressed any genuine feelings for him at all. Which meant she might not quite be ready to continue what they were doing without the stupid "arrangement" giving her the protection something deep in her psyche required her to have.

It appeared that while it might be good for the soul, confession might *not* yet be good for his relationship with the woman he was falling in love with.

So his mouth would stay shut. Even if his heart was wide-open.

10

THIS LAST WEEK before Tabitha's wedding was shaping up to be a crazy one and by Tuesday afternoon, Maddy was already completely exhausted. Not only because she'd had two long, glorious—and sleepless—nights in Jake's arms, but also because of the typical prewedding hysteria every family experienced.

Tabby was a mess. The bride had been worrying herself into a frenzy about the weather, the caterer, the vows, the rings. She'd second-guessed the brand of champagne, argued with the wedding planner and was stewing over her honeymoon trousseau. Not to mention, she was starving herself to fit into her size two dress.

Maddy had worn a size two once. When she *was* two.

Still, she didn't envy her sister one bit right now, and wouldn't change places with her for the world. Except, perhaps for one thing.

She did wonder what it might be like to be loved so deeply by a man.

Her sister's fiancé must love Tabby madly. It was the only explanation for why he'd put up with the antics of someone so totally unlike himself. Why he'd be drawn to his complete opposite. Love like that sounded *so* nice.

Who was she kidding? Being loved like that by a wonderful man sounded utterly amazing. Especially if the man was Jake.

Stupid. She had no business thinking that way, but the fantasies kept creeping up on her at the oddest times. Especially after she gave in and finally allowed herself to admit—after their conversation in the car Sunday night—that she *had* changed, as he'd pointed out. He simply didn't realize how *much* she'd changed.

She'd fallen in love with him. Against all her own cautionary advice and better judgment, her walls had dropped and her heart had filled.

While a big part of her wanted to tell him, another part—the sensible part—had known she couldn't. Not until their deal was finished, their thirty days up. After that, if Jake stayed, it would be for personal reasons only. She couldn't use her feelings to pressure him in any way.

And that was why she'd demanded that he cash that stupid check. They had to keep their arrangement, if only to make sure that whatever happened afterward, happened because he felt as deeply for her as she did for him.

"In love," she whispered under her breath Tuesday afternoon, after daydreaming her way through an executive meeting led by her father.

The ice queen had completely melted for a gigolo. Wouldn't the tabloids adore that.

"What did you say?" her father asked, obviously hearing her words, since only the two of them remained. The meeting had wrapped up a few minutes ago.

"Oh, nothing," she said. "Just thinking about the wedding."

"Of course, who isn't?"

Their father had been preening in his role of father of the bride, while also going over every detail with his keen businessman's eye…as well as inviting anyone he felt like asking. He had, in fact, extended two verbal invitations this very day.

"You know, Tabby's going to kill you. If those two California businessmen come this weekend, you're going to throw off her seating plans."

Her father frowned, thought about it, then winked. "I'll blame Deborah."

Their father was no dummy. He had absolutely no illusions about how his oldest daughter felt about his young wife. Yet he still managed to keep his sense of humor about it.

Tabby was right. He really did seem happy. So maybe he did genuinely love the woman.

Good grief, she must be turning into a complete mush-bag believing in all this true love involving *her* family.

"Do you really think our girl's going to be happy with that stick-in-the-mud Bradley?" her father asked, putting words to a question Maddy had considered a few times herself.

"She seems to be. She says he calms her."

Her father shrugged, not appearing convinced. "Calms her… or bores her?" Then he frowned. "I have heard rumors that he's a very rigid, strict man."

Knowing her sister, he would not stay that way for long. "It'll be fine. Besides, you know Tabby. She has no problem calling something off if it's not going to work out. And she's determined to go through with it."

He sighed, obviously remembering the money he'd paid for past engagements…and one lavish wedding. "So far." The way he glanced at the documents in his hands did not disguise his overly innocent tone when he asked, "And what about you, sweetheart? Is that handsome, dark-haired fellow escorting you?"

"Dad…"

"You can't blame me for being curious. He seems like a good sort."

"He is a good sort," she admitted, hearing a completely unfamiliar soft, mushy tone in her own voice. "In fact, he's wonderful."

Her father dropped his papers, reached for her and gave Maddy a quick hug, kissing her temple. "I can't tell you how thrilled I am to hear you say that." His eyes were suspiciously moist when he pulled away. "I want you to be happy, Madeline. And I'm *thrilled* to see you giving someone else a chance after what that vile bastard Oliver did."

One way to get her father riled up and send his blood pressure through the roof was to talk about her ex. "Forget him Dad, he's *nothing*. And yes, Jake is escorting me this weekend." Though she didn't want to get her father's hopes up about Maddy actually being involved in a real relationship—given Jake's profession—she did like seeing the shadow of worry disappear from his eyes. "I think you'll like him."

"I think I already do," he murmured, touching her cheek with sweet tenderness. "He brought that beautiful smile back to your face and the warm sparkle in your eyes. I've missed seeing them in the past eighteen months." He stared at her for a moment, as if memorizing her features, though he'd seen her nearly every day for her entire twenty-eight years. "You are so lovely, my dear," he mumbled, that moisture appearing in his eyes again.

Her father was behaving in a most un-Jason-Turner-like fashion today. Loving he may be—maudlin and sentimental he was not. This upcoming wedding must have really gotten him thinking, and worrying, about Maddy's single state.

"Love you, Dad."

"I love you, too." And as quickly as his odd mood had come over him, he shook it off and pointed an index finger at her. "Now, don't forget this evening. You know I'm counting on you to keep the peace."

Her usual role in the family.

"I won't forget," she murmured, wishing she *could.*

Her father had insisted on one last "family" dinner before things got too crazy. Which meant she'd be seeing her step-mother, the only person who did *not* seem to be going insane with wedding preparations, or to even be involved with them at all.

The woman had been avoiding her—and Tabitha, too—as if they both carried the Ebola virus. Maddy suspected she was too embarrassed to face her stepdaughters, having to know that they were both fully aware of why she'd been at that auction.

Tonight, though, Deborah could no longer escape. Neither, unfortunately, could Maddy or her sister.

Absolutely the only good thing about the evening, in Maddy's opinion, was that she would have the chance to warn her step-mother about who her escort would be, both at the rehearsal dinner and the wedding.

She didn't merely want to avoid any embarrassing moments that her father might pick up on. She also didn't want Jake subjected to any whispered come-ons. Frankly, the way she was feeling, if her stepmother made a move on the man Maddy had come to consider hers, she'd rip the woman's hair out by its platinum blond roots.

So much for the ice queen.

HAVING TO PICK UP some extra shifts to make up for the time off he'd need to escort Maddy both to tonight's rehearsal dinner and tomorrow afternoon's wedding, Jake found himself missing her like crazy after only the few days they'd spent apart. It was as if she was a drug to which he'd become completely addicted. And honestly, he'd never felt like that about anyone before in his life.

"You're losing it, man," he muttered that morning as he filled out some paperwork for a patient he and his partner had just brought in to the hospital. "Absolutely losing it."

And damn, didn't it feel fine. As long as, sooner or later, Maddy "lost it," too.

Seventy-two hours. That was far too long. He hadn't seen her since Tuesday morning, when she'd taken him back to his truck. It had been parked outside the same restaurant where they'd *tried* to dine Sunday night—before Jenny's interruption. They'd rescheduled for Monday, and had actually managed to complete an entire date. A *great* one, filled with laughter and good food, and more of that flirtatious banter Maddy seemed to want to try out—and was getting very good at. She was so adorably sexy to watch as she let her inhibitions fall away, one by one.

Speaking of sexy, that bridesmaid dress… Whew! While it had definitely lived up to all his heated expectations, he'd found himself dreading her actually wearing it to the wedding. He wasn't sure he was ready for the way other men were going to look at her, whether she believed that or not. The last thing he wanted to do was go off on a jealous rant in the middle of the fancy yacht club reception because some rich dickhead high on one-too-many glasses of champagne looked at her the wrong way.

She can take care of herself, he forced himself to acknowledge, remembering the drunk at the ball game.

"You finished?" the admitting nurse asked, interrupting his heated musings. Jeez, it wasn't often he got distracted from his job, especially with a case as serious as this one.

Maybe it was *because* this case was such a serious one. And because of the way the victim's wife had looked when she'd arrived here a few minutes ago.

Utterly and completely terrified.

Madeline Turner might not have seen a lot of true love in her lifetime, but oh, God, did it exist. Jake saw it every day—saw the anguish and the heartbreak that came with the thought of losing someone who was so deeply loved that their partner couldn't imagine life going on without them. Like the wife from this morning.

"Yeah, I'm done," he muttered. "Hope the guy makes it."

The patient he and his partner, Raoul, had brought in was a shooting victim, injured in an apparent home invasion. He'd been found unconscious on the floor of his own house. A neighbor had heard the shots and called 911. Jake and Raoul had arrived right behind the police and Jake's hands had been the first on the wounded man's bloody chest.

"I think he will."

Good. The guy was middle-aged, had a nice home and a loving wife who'd apparently just left for work when it had happened. He deserved a hell of a lot better than to die for opening his front door to the wrong stranger.

Though they needed to get back to the station, he and Raoul stuck around, both to keep an eye on the man's condition and because they'd already been told they'd probably have to give a statement to the police. This suspect was apparently one nasty character and the cops wanted him bad.

Raoul had gone to secure the truck and to radio the station that they were going to stay for a few minutes. Grabbing himself a cup of coffee from the lounge, Jake hung around the E.R. information desk, watching the clock, hoping the team of detectives showed up soon. There were EMTs back at the station, but he was the only actual paramedic on today.

Finally, a stocky, solid woman with short, iron-gray hair and a no-nonsense attitude approached him. "You Wallace?"

"I am."

"Detective Harriet Stiles." She flashed a badge. "My partner spotted yours out in the truck and he's taking his statement."

She began asking questions, routine stuff. Jake only wished he could actually be of some help. He spoke clearly and concisely, telling what little he knew, since he hadn't seen the assailant, just the victim lying on the floor.

When he finished, Detective Stiles nodded and snapped her notebook closed.

"All done?" a man's voice asked the officer.

Jake glanced up and saw that a dark-haired guy, solidly built, a few inches shorter than him, had joined them.

"Looks like it. You?"

"Uh-huh."

"Mr. Wallace, this is my partner, Detective Santori," the first officer told Jake.

"Good to meet you. Huh…Santori. That name is familiar."

The other man laughed softly. "There are a *lot* of us."

Jake suddenly remembered how he knew the name. The woman from the charity—the one who'd tried to help him track down Madeline. She'd been named Santori.

"I met a woman—Nicole Santori, maybe? It was at a charity auction a few weeks ago."

The other man stiffened, his jaw jutting out the tiniest bit. "Are you talking about my *wife,* Noelle? She founded the Give A Kid A Christmas program."

Suddenly realizing why the other man had tensed—since the wife had, he recalled, been very pretty—Jake put both hands up, in a universal no-harm, no-foul gesture. "Hey, no offense. I was only asking because I wanted to try to get a message to her. There was a major printing mix-up that night with the program."

Santori visibly relaxed. "She won't be happy to hear that."

"Look, it turned out okay—in fact, great—on my end."

"Spoken like a man in love," said Detective Stiles with a low snort. She didn't exactly look like the romantic type.

Hell, he probably was wearing some kind of sappy, guy-in-love grin. Frankly, though, Jake didn't give a crap. He *was* a sappy guy-in-love.

"Like I said, I'm fine. But I don't know how the bachelor who was mistaken for me—and got my bio—is feeling about it. Whoever 'won' him was expecting a blue collar rescue worker. And, uh, I really *don't* think that's who she got."

"I see," Santori said. His brown eyes twinkled. Noting the laugh lines on the detective's face, Jake sensed he was pretty laid-back, when he wasn't going all alpha in claiming his wife.

"Noelle told me about a few of the more high-maintenance guys who showed up that night."

Jake had no idea whether the real gigolo was high-maintenance or not. He only knew he probably wasn't the kind of man who'd offer a woman baseball and beer. So whoever he'd ended up with probably had quite a surprise on her hands.

"Anyway, I just wanted her to have a heads-up. We were numbers nineteen and twenty, I think."

"Got it. Thanks for letting me know, I'll be sure to pass it along." He extended his hand, and Jake shook it. "Good to meet you…Wallace, was it?"

Jake nodded.

"Well, I know my wife was thrilled at the money earned that night. It went a long way toward helping meet her annual goal." He grinned. "From the sound of it, you guys really went through the wringer."

Groaning, Jake confirmed that. "You have no idea. I now know what a brownie at a Weight Watchers meeting feels like."

Both the officers were grinning as they murmured their good-byes and turned to leave, though Jake knew their smiles wouldn't remain during the very long day ahead of them.

Before they'd gotten more than a few steps away, Jake remembered something. Something big. "Wait!" Reaching into his back pocket, he retrieved his wallet, digging out the folded piece of paper he'd stuck in there the day he and Maddy had gone sailing.

She'd *said* she didn't care what he did with the money….

"I have another contribution to make," he said, not hesitating for one second in doing what he knew was the right thing. He had, after all, promised her. "Can you get it to your wife?"

"Of course."

Borrowing a pen, Jake unfolded the check, looking at it for the very first time. He immediately realized what a good thing it was that he hadn't lost the thing, because Maddy had filled out the amount, but not the name. As if she wasn't sure whether he used a different one for "business" or was trying to hide the income. Great. The woman either thought he was a tax dodger or that he'd incorporated himself in the sex trade.

Then again, considering she thought he was a gigolo, he guessed he shouldn't be surprised.

Writing the name of the charity and grinning when he pictured Noelle Santori's face, he passed the check over. The detective took it and prepared to carelessly stuff it in his pocket.

"Uh…you might want to put that in your wallet or something."

"Oh?" Santori finally glanced at the front of the thing, noted the number of zeroes, and muttered, "Holy shit."

"It's genuine."

"I sure hope so. What kind of rat-brained idiot would try to pass off a bad check for needy kids to a cop?"

"I have been accused of being many things, but never a rat-brained idiot."

The partner, who'd peeked over Santori's shoulder at the check herself, whistled. "Nice."

Very nice. Very worthwhile. And now that the check had been lifted from his pocket, Jake felt *very* lighthearted—as though he'd lost thirty pounds.

Or thirty thousand.

THE WEDDING REHEARSAL started at seven, with the dinner taking place right afterward at a nice restaurant in one of the hotels owned by the groom's family. It was now five. They should be leaving any minute to get there, given Friday rush hour traffic in the city.

Instead, the minute Jake walked out of the elevator and into her place, Maddy jumped on him. Literally. She flew into his arms, wrapped her legs around his waist and began pressing wild, frantic kisses on his mouth.

"I've missed you so much," she whispered when she paused to take a breath—and let him take one.

"Ditto." Holding her around the waist with one arm, cupping her bottom with the other hand, he strode straight down the hall toward her bedroom. He kissed her jaw, the side of her neck. "We might be late."

"Tabby's never been on time for a thing in her life," Maddy replied, letting her silky, short bathrobe slip off her shoulders and down her arms. She could have gotten dressed for their evening, as Jake—in a dark blue suit and crisp white dress shirt and tie— had. Instead, as she'd begun pulling on the lingerie she'd bought to wear beneath her new cocktail dress, she'd only been able to picture Jake taking it off her. And so, she hadn't bothered to finish dressing. "She was an hour late to her first wedding."

Reaching her bedroom, Jake tossed her onto the middle of her bed, watching with glittering, heated avarice as the robe fell completely down, revealing her black lace bra, black garter belt and sheer stockings.

"Then I guess Tabby won't mind if we're just a few minutes late to her rehearsal."

Maddy lay back on the bed, one leg straight down, the other bent at the knee in invitation. With one hand resting on her stomach, the other brushing through long strands of her loose hair, she gave him a wicked glance that left no doubt about what she wanted. "*Just* a few minutes?"

"After three and a half days without you, I want at least that long inside you," Jake muttered as he took his jacket off and tossed it onto a chair. "Can we skip tonight altogether?"

She shook her head. "I wish. But I'm the maid of honor, remember?"

"So we…get a little satisfaction now, then come back here tonight and I'll do you until we have to leave tomorrow for the wedding."

She shivered at the roughness in his tone, which spoke of his ravenous need. "Deal."

Jake loosened the tie next, taking a whole lot longer than such a simple chore should take.

"Uh, *FYI?* You're going way too slow."

"I said a *little* satisfaction. Not an infinitesimal amount."

Just her luck. Even when desperate, the man had agonizing patience.

"Hurry up," she ordered, writhing on the bed.

"Not a chance. We're not so pressed for time that I'll rush through something I've been fantasizing about for days."

Fantasizing about her when they weren't together? That was nice to hear. But it didn't exactly do anything about the mad heat spiraling through her entire body. "Haven't you ever heard of a quickie?"

"Yeah. And I want one. Maybe tomorrow, at the reception." His eyebrows wagged. "Want to meet me in the coatroom?"

Oh, he was wicked. So wicked. Just the thought of it sent a thousand more hot tendrils of electricity straight between her thighs.

"That's incredibly tempting," she admitted, meaning it. "But knowing how hard it's going to be to get myself secure in my dress, I don't know that I'll be up for taking it off in the middle of the big event."

He reached for the top button of his dress shirt, unfastening it with slow deliberation before moving on, watching her watch him. "I'd be there to help you get…put back together."

After he sent her flying apart, no doubt.

"Unless you're going to pack a crowbar in your tux to squeeze everything back in, and strong tape to hold it all in place, I think that'll be impossible." As it was, she'd had to buy some ridiculous sticky contraptions that were supposed to give her some support. The thought of gluing plastic film to her breasts seemed utterly ridiculous, and she already dreaded it.

The alternative, however, was worse. No way was she going braless.

"Maybe I don't want you wearing that dress around other guys." A frown tugged that handsome brow down and he'd stopped unbuttoning.

Jealous? Was that even possible? A little thrill of excitement at the thought of it made her heart roll. "They'll *see* it. You'll be the only one *not* seeing it when I take it off."

"I suppose that'll have to do." He stared at her legs. The hose. The garter belt. The tiny black panties. "Getting back to our quickie. Maybe you wouldn't have to worry about your dress. Wear what you have on now." Smiling with pure heat, he added, "*Without* the panties. I'll lift your gown and take you right up against the wall of the closet, daring you not to scream."

She groaned, her legs clenching, ready to scream right now. "I'd lose that dare."

He seemed oblivious to her agony, still taking his own sweet time, arousing her word after word, look after look, not having even touched her since he dropped her onto the bed. But at least he resumed working on those double-damned buttons.

Picturing the interlude he'd proposed, she murmured, "Can you imagine trying to walk out of that coat closet into the reception and act normally afterward?"

"You're going to be doing it tonight at the dinner."

Confused, Maddy merely stared.

A look of such tenderness appeared on Jake's face, it took her breath away to think it was directed at her. "Oh, honey, you have no idea how you look after we've made love. You wear your happiness on your face for hours afterward."

Good Lord. Such sweet words. Had any man ever touched her with just a whisper the way this one had?

Easy to answer. Absolutely not.

"Tonight at the rehearsal you're going to have that soft smile on your face and that glow in your eyes. Your skin will be flushed and you'll be a little slow and dreamy in your movements, like your body is there, but every other part of you—heart, mind and soul—is right…back…here."

Maddy closed her eyes, not wanting him to see what she suspected lurked in them. The sheen of tears—and a whole lot of genuine emotion. Maybe even the love that she'd finally acknowledged, if only to herself, that she felt for the man.

Finally feeling capable of speaking—and looking at him—she opened them again. "Jake, I am so glad I met you."

"Me, too," he admitted.

Their stares met, exchanging unspoken emotion, and in that moment, Maddy knew their relationship had just moved up to something else. She wasn't sure what. Just something. And, to her complete surprise, she wasn't utterly terrified by that realization.

But there was no time to dwell on it now. Certainly not enough time for them to drag it out and talk about it.

Pursing her lips, Maddy focused her attention on his still-clothed body. "Ahem. Back to our time limits? If you don't get out of those clothes, I'm going to rip them off you."

"Then I'd have nothing to wear tonight," he said with a teasing shrug. "So I guess you'll have to be patient."

How could the man drive her so completely mad, yet still remain so in control, just now getting around to pulling his dress shirt off and tossing it aside? Here she was laid out like a *Penthouse* playmate, with the figure and the fantasy lingerie to back it up, and the guy hadn't even unfastened his belt.

"Is there *anything* I can do to make you go faster?"

He shook his head.

"Maybe I should start without you."

"Maybe you should."

That was a challenge. And maybe even a sexy plea.

Maddy accepted, sliding her hand up, letting her fingertips ease a slow, lazy path across her constrained breasts. She rubbed one nipple, already hard and sensitive against the black lace. Then she tugged one bra strap down, releasing her own sensitive mound for his perusal and her own touch.

He growled. And maybe the belt slid through the hoops of his trousers a teensy bit faster.

"Mmm," she murmured, sliding two fingers against her nipple, toying with it, plucking lightly.

Wanting to see more of that desperate want on his expression, she lowered the other bra strap, then twisted the bra around and unfastened it completely.

"You take my breath away every time I look at you," he whispered, devouring her with that gaze.

But the man still had his damn pants on.

"You know what I've always wanted to try, Jake?" she asked, toying with both peaks now.

"I'm afraid to ask."

Knowing how fascinated he was by her breasts, he had reason to be.

She sat up, scooted to the edge of the bed and let her stocking-clad legs part to wrap around his. The roughness of his trousers against the silkiness of the lingerie ratcheted up the level of sensation. Rough and soft, sweet and spicy.

Maddy reached for Jake's waistband, unbuttoned it, then slowly lowered his zipper. His rock-hard erection arched against her hand, but he didn't stop her. Instead, he watched with hooded eyes as if wondering what she was up to.

She'd pleasured him with her mouth many times and knew he loved it. She also knew it was what he expected.

It wasn't what he was going to get.

Tugging his briefs down and pushing them, with the trousers, over Jake's lean hips and butt, Maddy breathed lightly on that silky skin. But rather than taste him, she wiggled closer. Close enough for her nipples to brush against the fine hairs on his stomach, to feel the ragged pulse as his blood raged through his veins.

"Good God," he said with a groan, finally understanding her intention.

Reaching around to clench his taut butt, Maddy hugged him closer, smothering his erection between her full breasts, making a nice, soft, warm channel for him. He was helpless to resist, his muscles flexing in her hands, his pelvis tilting, his staff gliding against her body as if he was buried inside her.

"Maddy," he groaned. He twined his fingers in her hair and she looked up at him, wetting her lips, groaning in pleasure as he continued his slow, lazy thrusts.

"I never imagined how good this could feel," she whispered, admitting she was trying something new.

That realization seemed to make him grow even more engorged against her, and he threw his head back, the cords of muscle standing out in his neck.

Maddy wasn't entirely sure how far this kind of thing could go. Knowing Jake, he wasn't anywhere near coming. Nor was she selfless enough to give up truly having him inside her. But she did like it. A lot. She especially liked that he was visibly losing a little of that infamous control, his hands clenched tightly in her hair, his breath coming in short gasps.

"Gotta have the real thing, babe," he muttered, dropping his hand to her shoulders and pushing her onto her back.

"I wish you would," she whispered, wanting him desperately.

But instead of pushing her farther back on the bed and climbing on top of her, Jake remained standing between her parted thighs. He grabbed a condom out of his pants pocket, opened it and put it on between one breath and the next.

Unfastening her garters with a few easy flicks of his fingers, he reached for her panties and tugged them down, tossing them out of his way, then sliding his fingers into her silky wet body.

He seemed to lose the last vestiges of control at finding her already fully aroused and ready to take him. "I can't believe I'm doing this without giving you more," he said, sounding on the verge of desperation.

"Please, just *take* me," she groaned.

He didn't make her beg again. Jake lifted her legs completely until her calves rested on his huge, bare shoulders. Holding her hips and lifting her wet, tender core toward him, he plunged into her with sudden, shocking force.

Maddy screamed at the power of it, so filled by him she didn't think she'd ever feel whole again if he stopped making love to her.

He froze. "Maddy? You okay?"

One hand moved to her face, his thumb tracing her parted lips. She bit it lightly, already rocking up toward him, greedily demanding more as he began to pull away. "As long as you're not stopping, I am just fine."

"Then I guess I'm not stopping."

He pulled out, thrust again, the firmness of the floor beneath his feet giving him incredible control. Maddy was helpless to do anything but love every stroke, to gasp when he went fast, to whimper when he slowed down.

And finally, when he reached between their bodies and caressed her swollen clit, to cry out her release moments before he attained his.

Only then did he scoot her back and fall on top of her, both of them falling into a sudden and unexpected sleep, still joined in every single way.

11

THEY WERE LATE. Quite a bit late, considering they'd fallen asleep and hadn't awoken until twenty minutes before the rehearsal start time. Jake had made up as much time as he could behind the wheel of Maddy's car, but they still pulled into the church parking lot not a minute before seven forty-five.

"Oh, damn," Maddy whispered, seeing all the cars. Then, in a hopeful tone, she added, "I don't see Tabby's convertible. Maybe she's not here yet."

Or maybe she'd ridden with her father, her fiancé, or any other member of the bridal party, he thought. Not that he said so aloud.

When they got inside and saw Maddy's very anxious father rushing toward them with an expectant expression, he figured Maddy had been right.

"Is Tabitha with you?"

"No, she's not." Maddy glanced toward the group of people clustered at the front of the church, then back at the closed doors through which they'd just come.

"Please tell me your sister isn't going to do this again."

"Again?" Jake whispered before remembering the previous wedding, and the previous broken engagement. Or engagements?

"Have you called her?" Maddy asked.

"I have. Everybody has."

"Where's Bradley?"

"He was late, too," Jason Turner said. Finally noticing Jake's presence, the man offered him a friendly smile, appearing pleased to see Maddy on his arm, despite his anxiety. "He arrived fifteen minutes ago and went right into the minister's office without talking to anyone, not even his parents."

Sounded unusual. Jake's senses went on alert. But when he heard the door behind them open, and saw the relieved look on Jason Turner's face—and on Maddy's—he figured maybe his instincts were slightly off. This time.

"I'm so sorry!" exclaimed the bride, a tall, slim blonde, who looked about as much like Maddy as *he* resembled George of the Jungle—the cartoon one. "There was an issue with the lobster for tomorrow, then I had to deal with some problems with the fountains and the fireworks."

Yeesh. Lobster, fountains and fireworks. Was this a wedding or a state dinner?

"Bradley *is* here?" she asked, her tone hardening.

"Yes, of course," her father said, taking her arm to lead her to the front of the church. "Don't worry, he was late, too."

"I know," the woman said.

Seeing the way Tabitha's spine stiffened, her shoulders squared and her head came up, as if she was preparing herself for an ordeal, he couldn't help wondering at the not-so-happy bride's mood. It seemed to be more than simply annoyance.

Neither her father nor her sister, who both appeared relieved, even noticed. Especially not when the bride swept toward the front of the church, expecting—and getting—the small crowd to part in front of her.

Yeah. About what he'd anticipated, from all Maddy had said. Tabby seemed to be exactly the self-absorbed woman he'd pictured. She'd probably kept everyone waiting intentionally, just so she could make her grand entrance.

Throughout the brief rehearsal, though, as he watched from the back of the church, he began to wonder about those strained undercurrents he couldn't help noticing. Not from everyone. Maddy seemed fine—more than fine, in fact. She was beautiful, still flushed from the love they'd made, as he'd known she would be. She also appeared genuinely happy for her sister, and made a stunning picture as she walked down the aisle.

God, the *images* that put in his head. Even if being here, among all these rich people who probably made his annual salary in a day, should have him running the other way.

Damn it, they could work it out. He loved Maddy. He suspected she loved him, too. That was all that mattered—it was the *only* thing that mattered. He just needed to keep reminding himself of it.

Though Jake's attention remained on the woman he'd escorted here tonight, he definitely felt some vibes coming off the engaged couple. Tabitha's laughter seemed almost too bright, her mood more forced than joyous. And the groom had little or nothing to say at all.

Yeah. There were definitely some undercurrents going on, though maybe they were only visible to an outsider who didn't have anything at stake in tomorrow's high-society event.

In the car, on the way to the dinner, he voiced his observations to Maddy.

"What? Are you kidding? Tabitha's very happy."

That hadn't seemed like happiness to him. Then again, maybe for Maddy's sister, the tight smile was typical, maybe her eyes never sparkled, and the slight droop to her shoulders was a result of fatigue from wedding mania.

But he doubted it.

"I can't believe I forgot to even introduce you," she said, sounding genuinely distressed. "I'll rectify that as soon as we get to the hotel."

The one owned by the groom's father. He remembered that

tidbit. "Yeah, be sure to point out your stepmother, too, okay? I want to make sure I'm ready to deal with her…just in case."

"I told you, I already warned her you'd be there."

She had, on the way to the church. Fortunately, it hadn't been an issue then, because the stepmother of the bride hadn't bothered to attend. Another tidbit that caused the bride's mouth to tighten. Deborah was, however, per Maddy's father, definitely going to be at dinner.

Yippee.

"She and I didn't have time to talk for more than a few minutes the other night, but I put her on notice." Maddy's mouth tightened. "There's no way she's going to say anything my dad might overhear. That would put her in some serious trouble."

"I know," he mumbled, though his mind had already shifted gears. He didn't give a rat's ass about Maddy's stepmother, beyond the fact that he wouldn't want Jason Turner, whom he already liked, hurt in any way.

Nor did he give a damn what anybody else—the stepmother, or any of the spoiled, rich socialites who might show up at the wedding tomorrow and remember him from the auction— thought of him. They could consider him the biggest boy toy in the world. It didn't matter. Only one person's opinion mattered and she was sitting right beside him.

Maddy deserved the truth; he had known that for days. But it had never been more clear to him than those moments before he'd made love to her tonight, when their eyes had met and they'd silently said the words that neither of them had dared to voice out loud.

He loved her. There were no more caveats, no more qualifications, no more maybes. He couldn't hide behind the protective, halfhearted idea that he was "falling for her" or that he *sensed* they could have something, or that he *thought* he could love her. He did love her. Period.

And her expression tonight, not to mention every moment they'd shared in the past several days, told him she loved him, too. Whether she loved him enough to get over the fact that he'd let her believe a lie, he didn't know. All he knew was that, feeling the way he did, he couldn't continue something he found so morally dishonest. Even though they were almost to the hotel and there was really no time, he found he could no longer continue the charade. He couldn't walk into that dinner filled with her family and friends under such dishonest terms.

"I need to talk to you, Maddy," he murmured, his eyes on the road. "Before we get there, you have to know a few things."

She stiffened in her seat. He didn't have to see to know it, the air in the car changed with her sudden tension. God love the woman, she was so used to having the rug yanked out from under her, she'd probably been steeling herself for something to happen. Something bad.

He tried to keep things light at first. "I hope you have money in your account, because your check is going to clear your bank any day."

She let out her breath in an audible whoosh, which, considering she'd just gone through a whole lot of money, said a lot about how dark her expectations had been. "Okay." Laughing lightly, she added, "It's certainly not going to bounce."

As if. "Be sure you hold on to the canceled check. You're going to need it come tax time."

"Why?" Her hand moved to his leg. "Do they allow deductions for, uh, *this,* now?"

He covered her fingers with his, lifting them to his mouth to press a kiss there. "No. Because I signed it over to the Give A Kid A Christmas people."

Her fingers tensed against his mouth, but she didn't pull away. *Oh, sweet Maddy.* He knew what she was thinking, what she was wondering. Should she be angry? Should she be hopeful?

"I told you to do whatever you wanted with it." She didn't sound cold, merely alert, knowing, already, that there was more.

"There's no way in hell I'd take money to be with you."

"Jake..."

He cut her off. "Let me clarify. There's no way I'd ever take money to be with *any* woman. But especially not you."

At that, she did pull her hand away. They'd reached a stop-light a few blocks from the hotel, and he chanced a glance at her. Maddy was watching, her brow furrowed in confusion, her body tense. "I'm not following you."

So he told her. "I'm not who you think I am. I don't know how it happened, but somebody messed up at that auction. I'm not bachelor nineteen, I'm number twenty."

"What?"

"I mean, I know I *was* nineteenth. But it wasn't my bio that was printed beneath my picture in the program. It wasn't my life. I'm not the man you went there that night to find." Ignoring the fact that the light had turned green, he urged her to understand. "It wasn't *me,* Maddy."

It took her a few seconds. When understanding did wash over her, it did so instantaneously, and she gasped out loud, her jaw falling open. "Oh, my God."

"Yeah."

"You're not..."

"No."

"I mistook you for..."

"Uh-huh."

"Is your name Jake Wallace?" She still sounded dazed.

"Of course. I am the man you've gotten to know since that night. The only thing you don't know is that I'm a paramedic for the city of Chicago...not an 'international playboy and lover of women.'" *Or a hooker.*

Behind them, someone honked a horn, and he finally acknowledged that he'd been holding up traffic. He eased forward, spying the tall, high-rise hotel just ahead of them. Maddy remained silent, slumped back in her seat as he pulled into the parking garage rather than heading for the valet stand.

They weren't finished. They'd been late to the rehearsal, they could be late to dinner, as well.

Maddy waited until they were tucked into a small-car spot in the basement garage before she came back at him with the accusation he'd been expecting. "You lied to me."

"I know." He had no defense.

"You let me believe it. Let me make a fool of myself and assume horrible things about you."

He reached for her, but she jerked away. "I *know*. But not from the very beginning. Call me dense, but it wasn't until I went to meet you at the boat, and you explained how you 'knew' everything about me that I realized what the hell was going on."

Finally appearing more anguished than angry, she murmured, "I'm so sorry. God, how horribly offensive. How demanding and spoiled I must have sounded."

"Believe me, that first morning, those things you said…I was about as mad as I've ever been in my life. Not to mention stunned when you put forth your proposal that day on the boat. Right up until you told me who you assumed I was, and why."

"And then? What happened then?" she asked, coming to the most important part. The part where he'd have to make her understand why he'd done it, *and* make her believe in his genuine feelings now.

But before he could open his mouth to say a single word, someone tapped on the passenger side window. Surprised, Jake and Maddy both looked out and saw the bride herself, nibbling the corner of her mouth, looking unsure and unhappy and utterly unlike a woman about to marry the man of her dreams.

"Damn," he said. "We need to finish this conversation."

"I know."

"Can you tell her we need a few more minutes?"

Maddy pushed the button and lowered her window. "Hi, Tabby. Can you give us—"

"I need to talk to you."

Oh, boy. He sensed the bride was about to confess something. She looked jittery and nervous, obviously upset, more on edge than she'd been at the church.

"I am so sorry, Maddy, but there are two people upstairs who you are *not* going to want to see." She glanced across the car, saw Jake, gave him a brief smile, then focused on her sister again. "I could wring my future father-in-law's neck. I've been watching for your car so I could give you a heads-up. I'm really glad you guys decided to park down here so we have a minute."

"What's wrong? Who is upstairs?"

"Bitsy."

"Ick."

"I know. She was having dinner in the restaurant. I guess she knows Bradley's family. Anyway, Mr. Kent spotted her, and invited her to join the party, which, of course, delighted Deborah."

Maddy glanced at Jake. "Bitsy is one of my stepmother's cronies. She, uh, was there. *That* night."

"Oh, this just gets better and better," he mumbled.

"No, it gets worse," Tabitha snapped. "Because Bitsy wasn't alone. She was with a date, the old skank. None of us realized who it was until they'd sat down. I told Bradley to get rid of them." She shook her head. "But he said Bitsy's family and his had been friends for years and he wouldn't do something so rude." She looked away. "Not even when I begged him to."

Jake sensed Tabby was hurt by her fiancé's refusal to back her up—which made him actually start to like her, maybe a little. At least for looking out for Maddy. The one thing he *didn't* get yet was who this unwanted second person was.

"I bet the witch did it on purpose," Tabitha muttered. "I can't imagine she didn't know our rehearsal dinner was being held here. And there is absolutely nothing she likes better than stirring up trouble and sitting back to watch the explosion."

Maddy was obviously losing patience. "Did what? Who is she with, Tabby? Would you just spit it out?"

"It's Oliver, Maddy. He and Bitsy are sitting right upstairs in the restaurant, where everyone is waiting for you—both of you— to join us."

AS JAKE LED HER toward the elevator a few minutes later, after Tabitha's shocking announcement, Maddy felt him silently offering support, even though he, himself, was tense and angry, obviously ready for trouble and spoiling for a fight.

"I know you probably don't want me around right now," he said, his tone gravelly, his jaw stiff. "But I'm not letting you walk into the lion's den alone. We'll finish our conversation the minute it's over."

He'd been keeping his voice low, to prevent Tabby, who walked a few feet ahead of them, from overhearing.

"I do want you around, Jake." *So much it scares me*.

She admitted it to herself—but not yet to him. She couldn't give him that much power, not yet, not until they had finished their conversation. Though she suspected he'd assume she wanted him there for support, tonight, that wasn't it.

She just wanted him in her life. Despite everything.

Maybe, even *because* of everything. Because Maddy could not deny that, while mortified and angry, she was also more than a little relieved that Jake *hadn't* stuck around for money. He had never, in fact, taken money from any woman. And falling hard for a great guy who saved people was a whole lot easier on her heart than falling for one who had sex for cash.

Maybe he really could be the man of her dreams.

But he's also a man who lied. So don't get your hopes up.

"I can hardly wait to see this bastard."

"I don't give a damn about Oliver. He's nothing." Frowning, she added, "And don't for one minute think you need to 'protect me.' The man is not worth the breath it would take to tell him off."

"We'll see," he muttered.

Caveman. The act was still kind of cute, if entirely unnecessary. Maddy could handle her ex. She could handle just about anything.

Except Jake walking away from her. Especially before she'd found out everything she needed to know.

"You doing okay?"

He wasn't referring to Oliver and they both knew it.

"I still want an explanation," she whispered. "And we will have that conversation. But I can't hate you when the whole thing started because of my stupid family dramas and a complete mis-understanding."

It was true. She was humiliated that he'd let her believe she'd "bought" him for a month. She definitely wanted to know why. But how could she stay angry when he'd made her happier in the past two weeks than she'd ever been in her life?

Seeing her sister reach the elevator and impatiently punch the up button, Maddy put a hand on Jake's sleeve, stopping him, and turned to look up at him. He watched her with tender eyes, a loving expression. *Loving.*

He hadn't said it. He hadn't claimed that's what had driven him to pose as—oh, God, she still couldn't believe the whole nightmarish mix-up had happened—a gigolo. This wonderful, funny, thoughtful, laid-back all-American family guy. What in the hell had she been smoking to believe his supposed vocation for one minute once she'd gotten to know him?

Once she'd started to love him.

"Thank you for telling me the truth. For not waiting until the end of the thirty days."

"I'm sorry I waited thirteen," he admitted. Jake lifted a hand to her face. He touched her cheek, brushed his fingers through her hair, even rubbed the side of his thumb along her eyebrow, as if wanting to memorize it. "Thank you for not kicking me out of your life. I..."

"Are you two going to stand there and make out or are you coming?"

Maddy sighed heavily, saw her impatient sister peering at them from inside the elevator, holding the door open with one slim hand, and forced a smile. "Tonight," she told him as they resumed walking. "Tonight, everything comes out. No more secrets. Then we see what we're going to do about it."

For the first time since he'd started talking in the car, Jake appeared relaxed. Maybe even hopeful. "That's a date."

Then they walked into the elevator. Tabby's frown said she was still furious. Suspecting Tabby was hurt that Bradley hadn't backed her up, on this, of all nights, Maddy acknowledged exactly what they were facing upstairs.

Her sneaky, cheating, lying ex wasn't such a big deal, at least not for her. But there were also a few women who thought the man holding her arm was a hot body for sale.

"What a night," she said as the elevator rose.

"Yeah," he agreed.

"I don't suppose you'd forgive me if I bailed, huh?" she asked Tabby.

To her surprise, her sister's expression wasn't immediately indignant. Instead, Tabitha said, "I want you there. But I will understand if you're not able to handle the drama. I'd bolt, in your shoes."

"Oh, she can handle it. We can both handle it," Jake said. He dropped an arm across Maddy's shoulders and tugged her close, asserting his claim and announcing his protection. He smiled down at her. "We'd just rather not expend the energy dealing with people who mean absolutely nothing to us."

"I like him," Tabby said, smiling what looked like her first real smile all evening.

Considering her sister had been her partner in crime, Maddy figured she should know the truth, too. "By the way…Jake is not who we—the world, the women at that auction—thought he was."

Her sister smirked, not believing it.

"Doesn't matter, babe," Jake said.

"Yes, it does." Maddy continued, her no-nonsense tone finally getting her sister's attention. "There was a printing error in the programs. I think the 'international playboy' was the man who came last. Jake's a paramedic. A completely not-for-sale-at-any-price rescue worker." She smiled up at him, shocked at how wonderful it felt to say the words out loud. To acknowledge the truth, and indulge in the feelings it engendered.

"Oh, my God," Tabby said, "you're serious." Her blue eyes grew wide as saucers. "You mean…you offered…he's not a…"

"No," Jake said. "Definitely not."

"I am *so* sorry." Then she gave him a once-over. "You could be, though. You have to admit that."

Laughing, he brushed off the assessment. "Forget it, no apology necessary. I suspect being mistaken for some male hooker might have been the best thing that ever happened to me."

And to her.

She'd fallen in love with him when she'd thought he had a string of rich women following him around. Knowing he was a good-natured hero, well, just about every doubt she'd had about him had disappeared from her mind.

Just about. There was, of course, still that tiny whisper in the back of her brain, reminding her that she *knew* better than to believe in true love or happily ever after. Despite the fact that, right now at least, she felt surrounded by it.

Tabby loved her fiancé and he loved her. Dad loved his wife—okay, she didn't quite fit in the example because, as far as Maddy was concerned, Deborah was a bitch who didn't deserve him. But hopefully the woman had now been "scared straight" by her close call at the auction.

She hoped so. Her father certainly seemed to love the woman. He'd shown no signs that his attention was waning, even though they'd been married for a year and had dated for four years before that.

So maybe all the Turners were changing. Every one of them. Maybe even her.

They'd reached the lobby floor, and as Tabby led them out of the elevator, Maddy saw into the arched opening of the private room in the restaurant, and stiffened. Oliver was a rotten jerk to be here, when he knew she'd be coming. And she could not even fathom what her father must be feeling, knowing how utterly furious he became at even the mention of her ex's name.

"It'll be fine," Jake reminded her in a whisper.

"Stay close."

"I won't let him bother you."

"I don't give a damn about him," she muttered. "But if Bitsy Wellington puts a hand on you I might chop it off with a steak knife."

He threw his head back and laughed, all good humor and masculine sexiness, as they entered the restaurant.

Everyone stopped talking. Every older person—her father, her aunts, family friends—smiled, probably thinking Maddy had found the right man at last. And every single woman in the place almost certainly envied her.

She kept her arm wrapped tightly in his, silently staking her claim.

They were welcomed with a round of introductions, then quickly seated just before the dinner began. Breathing a sigh of relief that things had gone smoothly so far, Maddy took note of every detail, especially the layout of the room.

She strongly suspected there'd been some rearranging going

on before they'd arrived. She and Jake were not seated with the bridal party, but rather at a side table with a few family friends. One of her cousins and her husband sat near Maddy's father, in the direct line of sight of Bitsy and Oliver's table.

Oh, yes. Somebody had switched the name cards. Thank goodness.

Unfortunately, there had been no way out for Tabby, who cast such obvious glares at Oliver that it was amazing he hadn't had the sense—not to mention courtesy—to get up and leave. Then again, he certainly hadn't displayed either of those traits before tonight…why start now?

"I wonder how Dad's holding up," she whispered, her gaze continuing to return to the older man. He appeared fine on the surface, smiling and exchanging small talk with the parents of the groom. But Maddy had seen him cast more than a few hard stares in her ex's direction, and every time he did, his face went a shade redder.

"He doesn't look great," Jake replied. Then, his eyes narrowing, he craned his neck to peer around the small sea of people separating them from the head table. "The blonde, beside him, is that your stepmother?"

"In the flesh." Did that sound *too* sour?

"She looks familiar."

"She tried to buy you, remember?"

"It's something else…. Oh, God, now I remember." Jake leaned closer, obviously realizing his loud pronouncement had caught the attention of a few people around them. "She's the one who told me how to find you."

Maddy didn't understand.

"That night, after you left, I was trying to track you down. I told you a woman told me your name and where you worked."

"*Deborah?* Are you kidding? I figured it was Tabby!"

"It was Deborah, definitely."

How unexpected. Maybe pure embarrassment had led to the older woman's actions. It was the only explanation Maddy could come up with.

Glancing at the head table, she noted the stiff way her stepmother sat at her father's side. Deborah lifted her glass, stared into the ruby red-wine within it, then tossed it back, gesturing to the waiter for another.

So unhappy. So very unhappy.

Much, she had to admit, as her sister looked. Tabby, a few seats down, had a tight, forced smile on her lips. And while her chair was close to Bradley's, they didn't touch. Not at all.

"What the hell is going on here?" she whispered.

"I don't know. I just know she told me how to find you, So even though she tried to buy me like a side of beef, I'm ready to kiss the woman."

Maddy put her hand on Jake's forearm, which rested on the edge of the table. Smiling at one of the bridesmaids, who'd stared over in curiosity from the head table, Maddy warned, under her breath, "Do and you might be on the receiving end of that steak knife."

"Jealousy? That's a good sign, right?"

Maybe it was.

"I can't wait to get out of here," he admitted, and she knew he was not referring to the oddly tense celebration. "This is almost over, right?"

The waiters had cleared away the dinner dishes and were bringing dessert. The toasts and speeches had occurred before they'd arrived, and the wedding party gifts had been opened. So yes, thankfully, it was almost over. There hadn't been a single opportunity for Oliver or Bitsy to speak to them. If Maddy had her way, they'd be out of here before the two unwelcome guests ever got the chance.

"Absolutely."

For a few minutes, Maddy *thought* she'd have her way. As dessert ended and everyone prepared to leave, an impromptu receiving line formed at the exit. Tabby and her fiancé, as well as both sets of parents, were thanking their guests. The milling crowd, in no hurry to leave, lingered over each goodbye, blocking the door.

Groaning at the delay—for several reasons—Maddy remained silent as they edged closer to escape. Finally, there were only a few people between them and her father, who was at the closest end of the line. "Almost there," she whispered.

But they didn't make it. "Not going to even say hello?"

Oliver.

Maddy's back stiffened. She forced herself to pretend she hadn't heard, focused only on her father's face…not to mention the damned door.

Jake, however, did not. With his arm curved possessively around her waist, he glanced over his shoulder at the other man. "No. She's not. So shove off, will you?"

A grin tickling her lips, Maddy stepped closer, tempted to just push past the well-wishers and leave. Tabby would understand. But she wouldn't let this jerk force her out of her own sister's party.

"Oh, come on, Maddy, this is childish."

Feeling Jake tense, she murmured, "Forget it, he's not worth it."

Though as tall, her ex didn't even approach Jake's massive build. Which just proved he was a moron for what he did next.

"Jesus, Maddy, you won't even face me? Are you going to hide behind this hired stud all night?"

Gasping, she spun around, taking in both the sneer on Oliver's handsome face…and the spiteful amusement on Bitsy Wellington's. Obviously the woman—at least ten years Oliver's senior—had gotten what she came for. Nasty drama.

"Babe, like you said, he's not worth it," Jake murmured, putting

a hand on her shoulder. "Don't let him use me to get to you." He
raked a cold stare over Oliver's impeccably clad form. "I don't
give a shit what a lying, cheating little prick like this thinks."

Behind her, Maddy heard someone cough, or choke or laugh.
Dad. He'd heard. He'd edged closer. And he liked what Jake had
had to say. *Oh, God, what if he'd heard all of it?*

"You're right," she whispered quickly, tugging at Jake's arm.
They needed to get out of here. Now. "Let's go."

"You're the hired help, so keep your mouth shut," Oliver
said to Jake.

Oliver *must* have been drinking—he was flushed and there
was a definite slur in his voice. Not to mention that he seemed
to have lost his own sense of self-preservation if he didn't notice
that Jake, despite his casually insulting tone before, was holding
his temper in check by the merest sliver.

Still oblivious to the danger, Oliver added, "Come on, Maddy,
you could at least talk to me. I didn't know I'd screwed you up
so badly that you'd have to *pay* for it ever since. If I'd known
you were that much in love with me, I'd have tried harder to make
you forgive me."

Jake snapped. With an audible growl, he stepped away from
Maddy, grabbing Oliver by the front of his jacket. "Let's go.
Outside. Right now."

Bitsy shrieked, apparently realizing the vicious games she
played could occasionally turn around and bite her on the ass.
Others in the room froze and stared at the spectacle. Maddy
couldn't even find her vocal cords to stop what was about to
happen, partly because she was reeling from Oliver's offensive
accusation and partly because she was stunned at the raw
violence dripping off the sweetest, most tender man she knew.

"Get your hands off me. She pays you to fuck her, not to
protect her."

"You sonofabitch…" Jake's arm flew back in preparation, but

before he could land a punch, another man had pushed between his fist and Oliver's face.

Dad.

"Young man, you are the most rude, disgusting, foul little rodent I've ever met," Jason Turner yelled, his face reddening, spittle flying off his lips. "How dare you say such things about my daughter?"

"Maybe because they're true? Just ask her. Ask if she's not standing beside the male whore your own wife tried to nail not three weeks ago."

Oh, no. Oh, no, no, no!

Everything had spun out of control so quickly, Maddy hadn't even had time to process it. Her father's face was beet-red, his breath coming in hoarse gasps. Jake dived for Oliver, sending them both rolling to the floor, fists flying. Deborah came running, screaming at Bitsy, who cowered away. Tabby came, too, looking ready to kick Oliver's face in if Jake botched the job. Fat chance that. The groom grabbed the bride, hissing at her that she was embarrassing him, and his parents hurried over to watch in offended horror.

But Maddy had eyes only for her father, *oh God*, her *father*.

"Dad?" she whispered, reaching for him, watching his breaths grow choppier, his face grow redder.

Jason waved her off with a weak gesture, then his left arm fell to his side, his fingers spasming as his shoulder slumped. He lifted his other hand toward his chest, bending over double at the waist, audibly struggling to breathe.

"Daddy!" she yelled, grabbing for him as he began to fall.

Those not paying attention to the brawl began to whisper in worry as Maddy collapsed with her gray-haired father to the floor. She knelt beside him, touching his flushed face…suddenly realizing he was no longer gasping for breath.

No breath at all.

"No…Tabby!"

Her sister spun around, finally realizing what had happened. She threw off her fiancé's restraining hand and sprinted over. Deborah, too, her eyes widened in shock, her mouth hanging open in horror, knelt by her husband's side, oblivious to her designer dress and their audience. "Somebody do something. Call an ambulance, hurry," she wailed.

Maddy jerked her head up, tears coursing down her cheeks as the image of her father's breathless, lifeless form imprinted itself on her brain. Her eyes found Jake's, locked on him, not needing to say a word.

He didn't hesitate. "Everyone get out of the way," he shouted, shoving his way over and dropping to his knees.

"Don't touch him," Deborah said. "You'll make it worse."

Jake ignored her, ripping Maddy's father's shirt open, straight down the front, leaning down to listen to his chest.

"Does he know what he's doing?"

"Yes," Maddy assured the other woman. "This is what he does. His *real* job. He knows exactly what he's doing." Then she looked at Jake, already tilting her father's head back, blowing puffs of air into his mouth, then fisting his hands to administer compressions to the older man's chest.

"Please…" she whispered, for his ears alone.

She couldn't form any more words, nor did she need to. Jake understood, it went without saying.

There was absolutely nothing he wouldn't do to save her father's life.

12

KNOWING HOSPITAL procedures by rote, as well as being friendly with one of the guys on the rescue crew, Jake knew he would be able to keep Jason Turner's loved ones a lot more informed than the average family. So there was no way he was leaving them. No way he was leaving *her*.

Not when she so obviously needed him.

He drove all three Turner women to the hospital, in Mr. Turner's car. He'd expected to drive Maddy and her step-mother—but he'd been genuinely surprised by Tabby's decision to ride with them, as well.

If she were his fiancée, he wouldn't have let her leave his side. He'd have been holding her, reassuring her that everything would be all right—exactly as he'd been doing for Maddy since the on-duty rescuers had arrived and taken over. Instead, from what he'd heard, Tabby's fiancé had been anything but supportive. He had, in fact, ordered her to calm down. The frowning man had actually *scolded* her for her hysterical behavior toward the asshole who'd caused all of this—Oliver—who she'd lunged at after the ambulance crew had wheeled her father out of the restaurant.

Jake understood Tabitha's actions.

He did *not* understand the groom's reaction.

In the same position, Maddy might have retreated behind her icy, self-protective wall, but Tabitha had not. She'd screamed at her fiancé, shrieking that he was partially responsible for what had happened. She'd refused to ride with him, climbing in beside a tearful Deborah and a white-lipped Maddy instead.

"He'll be all right, won't he? Please say he'll be all right," Deborah said from the backseat. She'd been repeating those words in some variation since the moment Jake had pulled into traffic, driving fast, ignoring the speed limit as much as he safely could.

"I'm sure he will," he replied, again. "He had constant CPR from almost the second his heart stopped. The EMTs were able to immediately defibrillate him back into a rhythm and he had a decent pulse by the time they pulled out."

A thready one…not that he told them that. Because any pulse was better than if Jason Turner hadn't responded to defib at all and had to undergo CPR all the way to the hospital.

"Thank God," Deborah whispered.

"Yeah. But no thanks to *you*," Tabby snapped.

Jake sucked in a slow breath. He'd been expecting this— waiting for the moment when it would start. Maddy had been silent, her lips moving as if she were saying quiet prayers for her father. Tabby's shock had worn off—now she was looking for someone to blame. Make that someone *else* to blame, considering she'd already told off Oliver and yelled at her husband-to-be.

Man, was the woman unlike her sister.

"Tabitha, please don't," Maddy murmured from the front seat. Jake reached over and took her hand, squeezing it. He didn't want her going through any more stress right now.

He seconded her plea. "It's not the time."

"When *is* the time? After she buries him under the ground and puts on widow's black to go out and do her whoring around?"

"Shut up," Deborah said wearily. "I don't have to explain myself to you. You have no idea what you're talking about."

"Oh, you mean, my father *didn't* grab his chest and have a heart attack because he found out his loving wife of one year was screwing around on him?"

"It's not her fault," Maddy mumbled. "Dad can't stand the sight of Oliver. He was working himself up into a frenzy without a single word about Deborah."

Knowing Maddy, too, had to resent her stepmother, Jake found himself surprised by the defense. Then again, Maddy knew her sister better than anyone. Probably the only way to calm Tabitha down was to try to deflate her righteous anger.

"Bullshit. He didn't keel over until after Oliver announced to the entire room that Deborah was a cheat."

"He knows," Deborah murmured, still sounding tired—and not interested in fighting.

"What?" Maddy turned in her seat.

"Not that I'm a cheat. I'm not." With indescribable pain in her voice she added, "But he told me to feel free to become one." She met Jake's stare in the rearview mirror. "I'm sorry, I understand there was a mistake about your identity." Then she dropped her gaze. "Besides, it's not like I would have gone through with it. I saw the way you looked at him, Maddy."

"You told him where to find me," she murmured from the passenger seat.

The woman shrugged. "What can I say? Hopeless romantic, that's me." Then she spoiled it, adding, "I know your father's been worried about you. You're all he *ever* talks about. Madeline this, and Madeline that."

There was a hard note in her voice, though why she'd display more anger toward the quiet, crying stepdaughter than to the bitchy, screeching one, Jake couldn't possibly say.

"I hoped that if you found someone, got busy with some kind of personal life, maybe it would be one less thing he'd have to stress over. I was hoping he'd stop the incessant *worrying* about you."

So her goal hadn't been exactly selfless.

"You are so full of it," Tabby snapped. "Don't believe a word of it, Mad, this is all a pack of lies."

"I'm *not* a liar. I am a forty-four-year-old woman who hasn't had sex in months, whose husband encouraged her to go out and get it somewhere else because he's no longer interested."

Whoa, this conversation he did *not* want to be party to. Not that he had any way to escape from it.

Judging by Maddy's wide eyes and pale complexion, he didn't think she wanted to hear it, either. Now that the words had started, though, Deborah didn't seem in any hurry to shut her mouth. "Do you know what it's like to try to keep up the happy wife front when your father doesn't want to touch me?"

"You're crazy," Tabby said.

"It's true," Deborah told her. "The last time we had sex, he called me by another woman's name. And because I had the foolish, soft heartedness to be hurt by it, he's decided we shouldn't even bother trying to have *that* kind of marriage."

"He loves you," Maddy whispered.

"No, *dear*, he doesn't." Now there was no mistaking the dislike coming from the woman's mouth. Again, directed at Maddy rather than Tabitha, who'd just called her a nutcase. "He said he did, but *wanting* to be in love with someone is *not* the same as loving them. Your father has nothing in his heart for me beyond affection. He wants only companionship and an occasional dance partner." Her voice lowered to a whisper. "I thought it would be enough, a friendly but loveless marriage." Sighing deeply, she added, "Hell, maybe I thought I could change him, even though no other woman has been able to."

Maddy's eyes, already wet from previously shed tears, blinked rapidly. As if unaware she was doing it, she slid her fingers from his, clenching her hands in her lap.

He took no offense. Sex talk about a parent was bad enough. Hearing that parent might actually be so cold, loveless—well, he didn't even want to think what it might be like. For Maddy or for her sister.

"So don't go judging me," Deborah continued. He glanced in the rearview mirror, seeing that she was again talking to Tabitha. "Not when you're about to do the same thing."

"I don't know you're talking about."

"Of course you do, dear. Please don't pretend I'm wrong. I know what a couple pretending to be in love looks like. You and Bradley don't love each other. At least, in my marriage, *one* of us is in love."

"Tabby?" Madeline whispered, this time turning all the way around in her seat. She looked as though she'd been hit—again—for the dozenth time in an hour. The heartbreak he saw in her eyes hit *him* again, too. "That's not true. You love him. You do, don't you?"

Silence. When Jake cast a look back, he saw Tabitha staring stonily at her sister, tears still on her cheeks—ones she had shed for her father. Not any fresh ones for herself and the future she *had* apparently chosen.

"You told me…"

"I thought I loved him," the older Turner sister replied. "I wanted to. Mainly because I thought *he* loved *me* and I'd be crazy not to feel the same way." She glanced out the window. "His family business isn't doing well and he needs money. He told me two days ago—said it wasn't *honorable* for him to marry me without telling me about his financial situation."

Maddy didn't appear ready to concede the point. "Okay. He should have come clean sooner, but he *did* tell you. So he does love you, and wants you to be together on open, honest terms."

Her sister laughed softly. So, from the sound of it, did her stepmother. As if the two of them knew something basic, something undeniable, something Maddy hadn't yet figured out.

Goddamn it, if he had his way, she'd *never* figure it out. Or at least never believe it. Not what he sensed they were trying to tell her.

"No, he was just afraid I'd find out after the wedding and divorce him. He called me into a meeting with his parents where they all informed me it would be a wonderful match, that they found me eminently suitable, despite my, how did his mother call it? My high-spiritedness." She sniffed and Jake didn't have to look in the mirror again to see her tears.

"That witch," Maddy snapped. "And Bradley—he's a coward."

"Just a man," Deborah murmured. "Like any other man."

Oh, by all means, ignore me. I'm not here.

"I wasn't happy about the dishonesty."

"Can't imagine why not," the older woman murmured. "Who wouldn't want a relationship based on lies?"

"Shut up," Tabby snarled.

Maddy interceded again. "Why didn't you end things? *Do* you really love him?"

"No. But I conceded the point. I obviously can't trust my own emotions. And a logical, well-thought-out marriage sounded like a very good proposition to me. It still does."

"It's not," Deborah interjected.

"I'm talking to my *sister*."

Oh, how he hoped the claws didn't come out again.

Maddy shook her head. "Oh, no, Tabby you *can't*. Tell me you're not going through with this."

Before she could answer, they reached the hospital. Every woman in the car leaned forward, wearing expressions of fear and anxiety. Jake *almost* pulled into the emergency entrance, by habit, but remembered, at the last minute, to go to the front. "Go on inside," he told them. "I'll park and meet you."

Maddy barely spared him a glance. She still appeared shell-shocked, stunned from the revelations from their short but informative car ride.

He was worried about Jason Turner. Very worried. Right now, however, he could throttle the man's wife and daughter for having aired their personal dramas—and man-hate—on the night when he and Maddy had reached their own crisis point.

Before she got out of the car, he grabbed her hand, silently urging her to be strong. To not give in to the pessimism that had just been dumped on her head. "Maddy, I…"

"Thank you for driving us," she said, her eyes averted, her voice calm. "I have to go."

He didn't like her mood. Not one bit. But there was nothing he could do. Not now, not until she'd found out whether her father was going to live or die.

After that, however, he intended to finish the conversation they'd started before dinner. And to reverse any damage the two other women in her family had caused.

THAT NIGHT WAS one of the longest of Maddy's life. She, Tabitha and Deborah shared an uneasy truce in the hospital waiting room, while her father went into surgery.

A double bypass. And they hadn't even realized there was a single thing wrong with him, beyond occasional high blood pressure.

Fortunately, Jake kept them informed about what was happening. He served as a liaison between the medical staff and the family. Not to mention a comforting presence for Maddy.

She didn't, however, allow herself to lean on him *too* much. Because even while racked with worry for her father, she couldn't stop replaying the conversation on the ride over here. The awful revelations, the sadness, the bitterness.

All the happy thoughts she'd had twelve hours ago about how the Turners seemed to finally have come out from under their unlucky-in-love-curse…. Look at them now. Tabby and her father both freely admitting they weren't in love with the people they'd pledged—or planned to pledge—to love until death. What in heaven's name was *wrong* with her family?

And was it also wrong with *her?*

Bradley was with them. He'd arrived shortly after they had. Despite being a jackass, in her opinion, he'd at least offered whatever comfort he could to Tabby. Not exactly warm, he hadn't been a disapproving, judgmental cold fish, either.

Well, maybe a disapproving one, at least when he'd *first* been introduced to Jake. But the judgmental glint had finally disappeared from his eye.

"Hopefully the word will get out to everyone else, too," she told Jake when they had a private moment. "I'll do my best to make sure everyone knows Bitsy and Oliver were crazy. Considering everyone saw you save my father's life, only a fool would believe the story, anyway."

Which said a lot about Bradley, who *had* still believed it until confronted with a truth he couldn't deny—Jake's friendly interaction with the hospital staff, who knew him by name and by reputation.

"Don't worry about it. I don't care."

"I do. My family has done enough damage to you." She heard her own stiff, formal tone and half hated herself for it. But she couldn't bring herself to ease up. Because while part of her wanted desperately to just lean on him, fall into his arms and take whatever comfort he could offer, emotionally, she couldn't risk it.

He opened his mouth to argue, as if realizing she'd begun to draw away from him, to retreat behind the barrier that had safely guarded her heart for so long, but the door to the waiting room was suddenly pushed in. Spying the surgeon, one of the best in the city—who'd come to the hospital immediately when he'd found out about her father—they all leaped to their feet.

"The procedure went very well. While I don't want to be premature, I do think it's safe to say Mr. Turner is well on the road to recovery."

Those were all the words Maddy heard before slowly sinking back to her seat. The others hung avidly on every instruction, every detail the physician would provide. She didn't. She instead sent up thankful prayer after thankful prayer, wondering if her own personal guardian angel—the mother she'd always imagined was watching over her—had been listening.

Hearing they could not take turns visiting for several hours, they all decided to head home for what was left of the night. Only an hour or two of darkness remained. Soon it would be the dawn of Tabitha's long-awaited wedding day.

God, how life could change in an instant.

One of Deborah's friends—not Bitsy, the woman didn't have a death wish—had shown up and offered to drive her. And Tabitha left with her fiancé—obviously they had some decisions to make about the wedding.

Frankly, Maddy hoped her sister canceled the thing for good, rather than just postponing it until after their father recovered. But she sensed Tabby wouldn't. One way or another, Tabby would probably marry the man. Because, despite loathing Deborah enough to ignore her advice, Tabby would go through it.

Her sister seemed ready to believe there was no such thing as true love. And more, that maybe there was even something wrong with her—something wrong with *all* of them—that made them genuinely incapable of sustaining the emotion.

Maddy could have told her differently. Because she had absolutely no doubt she was in love with Jake.

For now. That was the problem. She loved him *now*.

As for tomorrow? Well, despite her hopes and her dreams and her wishes over the past few weeks, she had remembered the truth—she didn't believe in tomorrows and happily ever afters and love that lasted a lifetime.

Yes, she loved him right this minute. But next year? Five years from now? Had anyone she'd *ever* known loved a lifetime?

No. They hadn't. Maybe in Jake's world, not in hers. And the man was just too good to have to live with that uncertainty.

Which left her with only one horrible, heartbreaking option.

"You okay?" he asked after a long, quiet drive back to her building. The streets were deserted and the silence inside the car had been even louder than the one out of it.

"I'm fine," she said once he'd parked in her reserved spot. "Thank you for being there."

"I guess I should let you get upstairs and get some sleep. Want me to come back and pick you up later this morning to take you to the hospital?"

A simple question. The one he *didn't* ask, however, was the one they were both contemplating. *Did she want him to leave at all?*

"Jake, tell me why you agreed to let me 'hire' you for thirty days. Why didn't you tell me the truth?"

He smiled gently, reaching over to brush her hair back from her weary, tear-sore eyes. "Well, first, because you flat-out said you wouldn't have anything to do with me if I didn't take your check."

True.

"But also because I knew you'd never give me a chance to just date you like a normal guy. You'd have to keep control…guard yourself. Keep on pretending you were that untouchable ice queen."

He sounded so tender, so loving, despite describing her with a term she hadn't even thought of in reference to herself in days.

"I saw a chance to see if something real could happen between us, and I took it, fully intending to tell you the truth as soon as I thought you were ready to hear it."

"Today." She glanced at the dashboard clock. "Yesterday."

"Well, I don't know that I thought you were ready. But I did decide I needed to get it out in the open. I couldn't go on with it anymore, not once I was sure how I felt about you."

Maddy held her breath, wanting to stop him, afraid to hear

the words. More afraid not to hear them—to never hear them come out of this man's mouth at all.

She'd regret that until the day she died.

"I love you," he murmured, lightly touching her cheek, turning her face to make sure she met his eye. "I love you, Madeline, and I'm sorry I was dishonest."

She merely watched. She couldn't give the words back to him, even though they were screaming a chorus in her brain.

"Tonight was bad and I know what you're thinking. That you can't trust me, that maybe I lied to you for the same reasons Bradley lied to Tabitha, and came clean for the same reasons, too. But it isn't true. I *love* you."

There she stopped him. He was in no way like her sister's fiancé. She put her hand up, covering his mouth with her fingertips. "No. I don't think you're anything like him. I believe you." She couldn't deny him the rest of what she owed him. "And I forgive you. I know you didn't set out to make a fool of me, or hurt me in any way."

He hesitated, still waiting, so sexy-yet-vulnerable, holding out for the words she was not going to offer him.

They wouldn't come. Not now, not ever. Not when she had the power to hurt him…tomorrow, next year. And not when she knew she could be crushed into unrelenting sorrow for the remainder of her life if he ever did the one thing that could most hurt her, too—stop loving her.

"I forgive you, Jake. But I don't want to see you again."

13

CONSIDERING SHE WAS BACK at the hospital by 10 a.m. on Saturday, Maddy might as well have stayed there. If she hadn't left, if she'd just curled up on the lumpy sofa to wait until visiting hours, perhaps she could have delayed the inevitable moment when she'd had to rip her own heart out. Because that's what she'd done with every word she'd said to Jake in the predawn hours.

"I'm so sorry," she whispered, rubbing her hands over her weary eyes as she watched the clock in the hospital waiting area. Her father was allowed two brief visits per hour, starting at eleven. She was the first of her family to arrive, and she could have come in a little later. But what was the point? It wasn't as if she'd slept, nor had she been doing anything at home that she couldn't do here. Worrying. Crying. Regretting.

If her fears about her father hadn't kept her brain from emptying and her eyes from closing in the cold darkness of her room, her heartache over pushing Jake away would definitely have done the trick, anyway.

He hadn't been pushed easily. He'd tried hard to dissuade her from doing what they both knew she didn't really *want* to do. But in the end, with tears streaming down her face as she admitted she was too tired, too frightened and too confused to think straight, he'd let it go. Let her have her way.

Let her shove him out of her life.

Maddy was no fool. She knew he'd only left because he, too, was worried about her father—and Maddy's own state of mind. If not for that, she figured they'd still be down in the parking garage below her building, arguing about whether or not he really loved her—and would keep loving her.

And whether or not she could allow him to.

Funny, the one thing he hadn't even questioned had been *her* feelings. He took her love for him as an utter certainty, though the words had never come out of her mouth.

It didn't matter. There was no hiding how she felt. From him, from either of them. "But that's today," she reminded herself as she watched the clock ease closer to eleven.

Tomorrow, well, her heart could prove to be as fickle and arbitrary as everyone else's in her family. And Jake deserved more than that. So much more.

She loved him too much to ever want to hurt him that way. Even if *she* hurt every minute of every day for the rest of her life.

"You're here!" a woman's voice said.

Half fearing it would be Deborah, Maddy couldn't help sighing in relief when she saw Tabby's pinched, pale face. Rising, she took her sister in her arms and hugged her close, looking over her shoulder into the corridor beyond to make sure she had come alone. "Are you all right?"

Tabby nodded. "Fine."

They drew apart. "You don't look fine."

"Well, hell, of course I'm not fine. Are you?"

Maddy shook her head. "But he's going to be all right."

"I know." Tabby reached into her designer purse and plucked out a wad of tissues, offering one to Maddy taking one and then wiping under her own eyes. "Can you imagine? Puffy eyes in my wedding pictures?"

Maddy's jaw dropped open. "What are you talking about?"

Tabby lifted her chin, her lips quivering, then straightening into a calm line. "Bradley and his family want to proceed with the wedding this afternoon."

"No, you can't do that!"

"They say it's exactly what Daddy would want."

They were probably correct. But that didn't make it right.

"They also pointed out, quite correctly, that everything is paid for, food prepared, flowers in place. Dozens of relatives have already come in from out of town. And that Dad's own surgeon said he was going to be fine. He just won't be able to walk me down the aisle…this time."

This time. Somehow, Maddy had the feeling Tabby was repeating verbatim words someone else had said to her. And she suddenly wanted to hit that someone for dumping such pressure—and guilt—on her sister's slim shoulders.

"*Don't* marry him." The words had left Maddy's mouth without her brain becoming involved in the decision. Her sister hadn't asked for her advice—but she gave it anyway, unable to stop herself. "You know he won't make you happy. You know you don't love him."

"I loved my first husband, and I have loved men since. Maybe marrying someone I don't love is exactly the right thing to do." She ran a weary hand over her face, looking every bit as exhausted as Maddy felt. "It's for the best, Mad. I'm just not cut out for it, falling in love and staying in love. My father's daughter, I guess."

How could she argue that, when Maddy had tossed Jake out of her life for the same reason?

Before she could say any more, though, Tabitha glanced at the clock. "Come on, let's go. She can't bitch about us going in first if she didn't bother to show up on time."

Maddy didn't even have to ask who *she* was. It was 11 a.m., Deborah wasn't here, and nobody would keep them from their father's side.

Reaching his room and gingerly pushing the door open, Maddy held her breath. She expected him to look near death. Pale and exhausted, weak, stuck with wires and probes and surrounded by machines.

He *was* stuck with wires and probes and surrounded by machines, and he did look tired and pale…but not at all on the verge of death. Instead, as he saw them standing in the doorway, he smiled and slowly lifted a hand. "My girls."

They flew to his side and cried like babies. Both of them. The Ice Queen and the Rich Bitch, sitting on either side of their father, holding his hands and sobbing their eyes out.

Which he quickly got bored with. "Enough. I'm fine. Stop or you'll soak my sheets. If the nurses think I wet this bed, I'll never be able to show my face at a hospital fund-raiser again."

Sniffling, Maddy managed a smile.

"What's going on? I'm dying for news," he said, trying to sound normal, though his weakness was underscored by the softness of his voice and the lines of fatigue and pain on his face.

"Everything's fine," Maddy said.

"Absolutely fine," her sister agreed.

"The wedding?"

Tabby stared at him, and Maddy read the anguish there.

"You are going through with it, aren't you? Don't you dare let this—" her father waved to his own limp body "—stop you from proceeding." Then, looking up at the ceiling, rather than at the bride, he added, "*If* you really want to marry him at all, that is."

Tabby sucked in a surprised breath. Maddy, who'd known her father had been having doubts, did not.

"If you *don't,* feel free to use your old man's weak ticker as an excuse to get out of the whole mess."

Tabitha just stared, her eyes huge in her pale face, not saying a single word.

Dad didn't push it. "Poor Deborah, she's not here?"

"I'm sure she'll be here any minute," Maddy said. "We just took advantage of the fact that we beat her by a few seconds."

"Perhaps."

"She was very worried," Tabby admitted, albeit grudgingly.

"I'm sure she was." Closing his eyes and sinking deeper into the pillow, he mumbled, "Don't judge her…I've been quite unkind to that woman."

Remembering what their stepmother had said—about how her husband had encouraged her to go have an affair—Maddy could only exchange a stricken glance with Tabitha.

"Shh, it's okay." Tabby stroked her father's thinning gray hair.

"I don't love her, you see." His eyes closed, his words drifting into little more than a whisper, as if he was speaking more to himself than to them. "I'm not sure who said it, but it's true. The only thing worse than being in a loveless marriage is being in one where there is love on only one side. You'd think I'd have learned that by now."

"Stop it. She knew what she was doing," Maddy said, more worried about her father's health than her stepmother's emotions. "Besides, you *are* capable of love, Dad. Just look at *us*. There's no doubt in Tabby's mind, or in mine, that you love us every bit as much as we love you."

A different kind of love—but she wouldn't allow her father to wallow in self-recrimination, not when he needed to recover.

Her words seemed to surprise him. His eyes flew open. "Oh, of course I'm capable of love, darling." His frail hands slid across the thin hospital blanket, so he could grasp his hands around one of each of his daughters'. "I have loved greatly."

And often.

"That's the problem, you see," he added, his fingers loosening, as if the effort to clench their hands was too much. "Like many others in my family—your grandmother, who lived alone for decades, my brother, always looking for the one he foolishly let get away—I'm at the mercy of my own heart." He lightly tapped his chest. "Which is, perhaps, a bit weaker than I'd supposed."

"What are you saying?" Tabby asked, in visible confusion.

He smiled up at his oldest daughter, who shared his bright blue eyes. "I cared for your mother, but we were young. Neither of us went into it for the right reasons."

Tabitha nodded, conceding the point. "I know."

"And I quite enjoyed many relationships with others over the years." Then he glanced at Maddy and his eyes moistened, as if tears were threatening. "But the truth is, we Turners are only capable of one *real* love."

Maddy sucked in a breath. She'd never heard her father talk this way, not in her entire twenty-eight years. And while for a brief moment, she wondered if his medication had confused him, she had to acknowledge that his gaze was clear; his voice—though weak—held certainty and conviction.

"It's a blessing and a curse in our family, but it's true. We can only manage it once. One great love, never to be forgotten, never to be replaced, not even if we end up entirely alone." He reached up and brushed his shaking hand across Maddy's cheek. "You break my heart and you fill it, every time I look into your eyes and see her there."

And suddenly she understood the words he was saying. The truth he'd never admitted before. Her father wasn't guilty of loving too briefly, or too shallowly.

The greatest tragedy of his life was in having loved *so* much he could never say goodbye.

"You're doomed, I'm afraid, both of you. So be vigilant, listen to your heart," he said, sighing deeply. "And when you do, savor every moment, don't waste a second of it. I pray you won't be like me. I found the other half of my heart and have spent twenty-four years trying to fill the time until I can be with her again."

Tears flowed freely down Maddy's face. Of all the moments in her life when she'd regretted having lost her mother, this was the most poignant.

Their father reached for Tabby's hand again, regarding her with sad eyes. "You've found the wrong one, darling…again and again, trying so hard and hoping each time will be better than the last." Then he turned his attention to Maddy. "And you, my sweet girl, have closed yourself off completely, never allowing yourself to believe you'll *ever* find the right one."

"Oh, Dad," Maddy whispered, her heart breaking for him more with every word he spoke.

There was, she knew, one gift she could give him, to help ease his worry, perhaps to help him heal. Just one secret…but the most important one of Maddy's life. "You're wrong, you know."

He merely waited.

"I've already found him," she said, then bent to press a soft kiss on his forehead.

He stared at her, seeing the truth there. "I'm so glad," he whispered. "So very glad." Then he fell asleep, looking comfortable and relaxed as his breathing continued evenly, steadily.

Maddy and her sister stared at their father, then across his bed at each other. The shock and grief for the long, lonely years their father had endured had to have been written just as clearly on Maddy's face as it was on Tabitha's. And, from both of them, maybe even sadness for the women who'd hoped to refill the vast empty wells of his heart that, to this day, mourned for Magdalena.

A nurse intruded, informing them their time was up. They rose in unison; each bent to kiss their father's cheek before walking out of the room together.

"I've got to go," Tabby murmured, her voice having lost that anxiety—the sadness and guilt she'd been carrying when she'd arrived here this morning. "I have a wedding to cancel and a fiancé to jilt."

Unable to stop herself from smiling, Maddy grabbed her sister's hand. "Me, too. I've got three words to say to an amazing man."

The love of her life. She no longer had a single doubt about it. And she would make sure he didn't, either.

"HEY, WALLACE, somebody's here to see you!"

Jake looked up from the medical kit he'd been restocking in the supply room, surprised that one of the guys had come back here looking for him. He wasn't even supposed to be on duty today. He'd taken the day off for a woman who didn't trust him enough to let him escort her to a family wedding, much less to love her. But staring at the four walls of his apartment had soon driven him batty and he'd come to the station house, determined to do a little restocking and catch up on some paperwork.

"Who is it?"

The guy, one of the newer firefighters, wagged his eyebrows. And Jake knew.

He shoved the case of sterile bandages he'd been holding back into the storage closet, slammed the door shut, and strode out to the front of the station. Maddy stood right outside, her beautiful, dark hair shimmering in the brilliant June sunshine. Her arms wrapped around her waist, she was dressed, not in her wickedly sexy bridesmaid dress, but in a simple jean skirt and brightly colored blouse.

The wedding, he figured, must have been postponed. No surprise there. He couldn't imagine his own sister going through with her wedding if something happened to their father. But given the identity of the bride and groom, he hadn't been entirely sure.

"Hey," he said when he reached her side. "You all right?"

She tilted her head back and looked up at him, a gentle smile widening those beautiful lips. "I'm fine."

"Your father?"

"Fine, too."

Then they fell silent. She'd come here to say something—he didn't have it in him to work up the hope that it could be something he truly wanted to hear. That she was wrong—so wrong—to put those self-protective walls around herself again. That she knew he'd never hurt her and was ready to admit she loved him, too.

But she said nothing.

"I guess the wedding's been postponed?"

She shook her head.

"Oh. Do you, uh, still need an escort?"

"Yes," she murmured, then cleared her throat. "Yes. I need an escort."

He ran a frustrated hand through his hair. "I left my tux back at my apartment." Glancing at his watch, he said, "Look, I'll go get it and…"

"No," she said, putting her hand over his mouth to shut him up. "I don't need an escort to a wedding. It hasn't been postponed. Tabby called it off. For good."

Sounded like one of the smartest things that sister of hers had ever done.

Maddy traced the tip of her finger over his lips, then his jaw and on down his neck before confessing, "But I still want the next fourteen days you owe me."

"What?"

"And then I want fourteen *thousand* more."

The ground lurched beneath his feet. Or maybe it was just his heart flipping around in his chest. Because that had sounded an awful lot like…

"What I need is an escort for *life*. I want to be on your arm forever, Jake, and I want you on mine," Maddy admitted, all attempts to protect herself, evaporating under the bright summer sky. "I want you sleeping beside me and waking up beside me.

Walking with me, and holding me. Laughing with me, crying with me, and keeping me from ever freezing up into *that* woman again."

"I love *that* woman," he said. "I loved her from the beginning. And I love *this* one, too. I love every part of you, Madeline Turner."

Stepping closer, until her body brushed his, she sent all his nerve endings on alert, filling his head with her sweet scent and his ears with her tender words. "I love you, too."

Her whisper sent the world spinning again, everything falling into place, exactly where it belonged. Right and perfect and all he'd ever dreamed of.

Maddy rose on tiptoe. "I love you so much and I don't ever want to lose you." She smiled, such a sweet, heartbreaking smile. "I've finally allowed myself to believe it."

"I'm so glad," he whispered, bending to brush a soft kiss on her lips. She wrapped her arms around his neck, kissing him back, her tongue mating with his, oblivious to time and place and anybody around them.

When the kiss finally ended, she didn't pull away, remaining wrapped in his embrace. "You should know, I won't ever let you go. Even if the world ended tomorrow and we never saw each other again…*I will never let you go.*"

She didn't have to explain. He understood completely. They were joined now. Through emotion and words and soon, he knew, through vows and family. Joined for life.

"Maddy, didn't you learn that the night we met?" he asked with a teasing kiss to her jaw. "I'll never let you get away from me, either." Then all teasing faded. "I promise you."

"Well, then, I guess we have a deal," she said. Her eyes twinkled with merriment and utter happiness. "Because I know you're not a welsher."

He tilted his head back and laughed up at the sky. He was happier than he'd ever been, more sure of the two of them being together than of anything he'd ever done.

And he was grateful—*very* grateful—to Fate, or whoever it was that had made *him* the man she'd chosen that night.

The one she'd chosen for life.

* * * * *

*Wait! Aren't you dying to know what happened
to that* other *bachelor? The* real *gigolo?*

*Well bad boy Sean Murphy's got his supersexy,
superseductive hands full dealing with a feisty day care center
owner who's unlike any woman he has ever met.*

*Annie Davis might have gone shopping for a blue-collar date
to take home to meet the folks, but she ends up
with a mysterious, jaded Irishman who begins to teach
her everything this small-town girl doesn't* know *about
making love.*

Don't miss Annie and Sean's story....

HEATED RUSH
Book 2: THE WRONG BED: AGAIN AND AGAIN
Available next month.

The editors at Harlequin Blaze have never been afraid to push the limits—tempting readers with the forbidden, whetting their appetites with a wide variety of story lines. But now we're breaking the final barrier—the time barrier.

In July, watch for BOUND TO PLEASE by fan favorite Hope Tarr, Harlequin Blaze's first ever historical romance—a story that's truly Blaze-worthy in every sense.

Here's a sneak peek...

Brianna stretched out beside Ewan, languid as a cat, and promptly fell asleep. Midday sunshine streamed into the chamber, bathing her lovely, long-limbed body in golden light, the sea-scented breeze wafting inside to dry the damp red-gold tendrils curling about her flushed face. Propping himself up on one elbow, Ewan slid his gaze over her. She looked beautiful and whole, satisfied and sated, and altogether happier than he had so far seen her. A slight smile curved her beautiful lips as though she must be in the midst of a lovely dream. She'd molded her lush, lovely body to his and laid her head in the curve of his shoulder and settled in to sleep beside him. For the longest while he lay there turned toward her, content to watch her sleep, at near perfect peace.

Not wholly perfect, for she had yet to answer his marriage proposal. Still, she wanted to make a baby with him, and Ewan no longer viewed her plan as the travesty he once had. He wanted children—sons to carry on after him, though a bonny little daughter with flame-colored hair would be nice, too. But he also wanted more than to simply plant his seed and be on his way. He wanted to lie beside Brianna night upon night as she increased, rub soothing unguents into the swell of her belly, knead the ache from her back and make slow, gentle love to her. He wanted to hold his newly born child in his arms and look down into Brianna's tired but radiant face and blot the perspiration from her brow and be a husband to her in every way.

He gave her a gentle nudge. "Brie?"

"Hmm?"

She rolled onto her side and he captured her against his chest. One arm wrapped about her waist, he bent to her ear and asked, "Do you think we might have just made a baby?"

Her eyes remained closed, but he felt her tense against him. "I don't know. We'll have to wait and see."

He stroked his hand over the flat plane of her belly. "You're so small and tight it's hard to imagine you increasing."

"All women increase no matter how large or small they start out. I may not grow big as a croft, but I'll be big enough, though I have hopes I may not waddle like a duck, at least not too badly."

The reference to his fair-day teasing was not lost on him. He grinned. "Brianna MacLeod grown so large she must sit still for once in her life. I'll need the proof of my own eyes to believe it."

Despite their banter, he felt his spirits dip. Assuming they were so blessed, he wouldn't have the chance to see her thus. By then he would be long gone, restored to his clan according to the sad bargain they'd struck. He opened his mouth to ask her to marry him again and then clamped it closed, not wanting to spoil the moment, but the unspoken words weighed like a millstone on his heart.

The damnable bargain they'd struck was proving to be a devil's pact indeed.

* * * * *

*Will these two star-crossed lovers find their
sexily-ever-after?
Find out in BOUND TO PLEASE by Hope Tarr,
available in July
wherever Harlequin® Blaze™ books are sold.*

Harlequin Blaze marks new territory with its first historical novel!

For years readers have trusted the Harlequin Blaze series to entertain them with a variety of stories— Now Blaze is breaking down the final barrier— the time barrier!

Welcome to Blaze Historicals—all the sexiness you love in a Blaze novel, all the adventure of a historical romance. It's the best of both worlds!

Don't miss the first book in this exciting new miniseries:

BOUND TO PLEASE
by Hope Tarr

New laird Brianna MacLeod knows she can't protect her land or her people without a man by her side. So what else can she do—she kidnaps one! Only, she doesn't expect to find herself the one enslaved....

Available in July
wherever Harlequin books are sold.

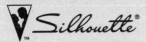

Silhouette®

Romantic
SUSPENSE

**Sparked by Danger,
Fueled by Passion.**

Conard County: The Next Generation

When he learns the truth about his father, military
man Ethan Parish is determined to reunite with his
long-lost family in Wyoming. On his way into town,
he clashes with policewoman Connie Halloran,
whose captivating beauty entices him. When
Connie's daughter is threatened, Ethan must use
his military skills to keep her safe. Together they
race against time to find the little girl and confront
the dangers inherent in family secrets.

Look for

A Soldier's Homecoming

by *New York Times*
bestselling author
Rachel Lee

Available in July wherever you buy books.

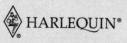

MADE IN TEXAS

It's the happiest day of Hannah Callahan's life
when she brings her new daughter home to Texas.
And Joe Daugherty would make a perfect father
to complete their unconventional family. But the
world-hopping writer never stays in one place
long enough. Can Joe trust in love enough to
finally get the family he's always wanted?

LOOK FOR

Hannah's Baby

BY

CATHY GILLEN THACKER

Available July
wherever you buy books.

LOVE, HOME & HAPPINESS

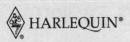

REQUEST YOUR FREE BOOKS!

2 FREE NOVELS PLUS 2 FREE GIFTS!

HARLEQUIN®

Blaze™

Red-hot reads!

Silhouette®

Desire

HIGH-SOCIETY
SECRET PREGNANCY

Park Avenue Scandals

Self-made millionaire Max Rolland had given
up on love until he meets socialite fundraiser
Julia Prentice. After their encounter Julia finds
herself pregnant, but a mysterious blackmailer
threatens to use this surprise pregnancy and ruin
his reputation. Max must decide whether to turn
his back on the woman carrying his child or risk
everything, including his heart....

**Don't miss the next installment of
the Park Avenue Scandals series—
Front Page Engagement
by Laura Wright—
coming in August 2008
from Silhouette Desire!**

Always Powerful, Passionate and Provocative.

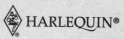

HARLEQUIN®

Blaze™

COMING NEXT MONTH

#405 WHAT I DID ON MY SUMMER VACATION
Thea Divine, Debbi Rawlins, Samantha Hunter
A Sizzling Summer Collection
Three single women end up with a fling worth writing about in this Blazing summer collection. Whether they spend their time in the city, in the woods or at the beach, their reports are bound to be strictly X-rated!

#406 INCOGNITO Kate Hoffmann
Forbidden Fantasies
Haven't you ever wished you could be someone else? Lily Hart has. So when she's mistaken for a promiscuous celebrity, she jumps at the chance to live out the erotic lifestyle she's always envied. After all, nobody will find out. Or will they?

#407 BOUND TO PLEASE Hope Tarr
Blaze Historicals
Blaze marks new territory with its first historical novel! New laird Brianna MacLeod knows she can't protect her land or her people without a man by her side. So, she kidnaps one! Only, she never expects to find herself the one enslaved....

#408 HEATED RUSH Leslie Kelly
The Wrong Bed: Again and Again
Annie Davis is in trouble. Her big family reunion is looming, and she needs a stand-in man—fast. Her solution? Bachelor number twenty at the charity bachelor auction. But there's more to her rent-a-date than meets the eye....

#409 BED ON ARRIVAL Kelley St. John
The Sexth Sense
Jenee Vicknair is keeping a wicked secret. Every night she has wild, mind-blowing sex with a perfect stranger. They never exchange words—their bodies say everything that needs to be said. If only her lover didn't vanish into thin air the moment the satisfaction was over....

#410 FLASHPOINT Jill Shalvis
American Heroes: The Firefighters
Zach Thomas might put out fires for a living, but when the sexy firefighter meets EMT Brooke O'Brian, all he wants to do is stoke her flames. Still, can Brooke count on him to take the heat if the sparks between them flare out of control?

www.eHarlequin.com